AN ODD COLLECTION OF TALES

CYE THOMAS

First Edition
Published by
Breaking Rules Publishing Europe, 2021.
This is a work of fiction. Similarities to real people,
places,or events are entirely coincidental.
Cover image by M.K Ragab at MK4© Designs
An Odd Collection of Tales
Cye Thomas
978-91-986841-3-1

TALES

AFTER

The bitter winter chill had descended quickly leaving the seaside town of Whitstable practically empty. As the last warming rays of summer were pushed back by the icy hands of a freezing southerly wind, the few hardy tourists that had battled it out had all but been driven away. Those few that now remained avoided the beach and headed into the brace outlets still open, gambling away the last of their holiday money as they sheltered from the freezing temperatures outside.

Although the retail owners hated the onset

of winter due to the slowing of trade, one local, Dylan Forkes, was unusually happy. The arrival of the new season meant a return to normality, a time to claw back lost freedoms and revel in the new solitude that the empty streets provided. Winter was a time to rejoice, it was a time to be clean again.

Slipping into a heavy coat, Dylan left his flat and headed down to the paper shop on the sea-front. Avoiding the eyes of the other two customers inside the store, he took a jar of coffee and a copy of the local rag from the shelf and paid the owner. Once the old man had growled something unintelligible and thrown Dylan's change at him, he headed back outside, taking the same route that he had arrived. As he scuppered along, the stinging sea breeze lashed at his body ripping at his exposed skin like a punisher's whip. Dylan didn't care. Buttoning his jacket tighter, he smiled and hummed a tune to himself.

As Dylan dipped his head against the wind, he noticed an object lying in the gutter by the side of the road. The object was black and shiny with a completely smooth surface. It was bigger than a pebble, but smaller than a cobble and seemed out of place by the drain that it lay beside. Staring down at it, Dylan wondered why it had not already been picked up. Someone must have dropped it, he decided. Perhaps it was a gift for a person who collected such things. Whatever it was, wherever it had come from, it was his now. He certainly did not intend to leave it lying there.

Stepping off from the kerb and ignoring the stinging breeze, Dylan scooped to pick up the stone. As his fingers touched the surface, he pulled his hand away quickly. It was hot, way too hot to touch. It was almost as if the thing had just come out of an oven.

Curious as to why the stone was emitting such heat, Dylan paused. He crouched down lower, completely mesmerised by its strange beauty. As he hovered, with half his body hanging dangerously over the road, a strange feeling began to build inside his head. Bizarre as the thought was, it almost felt as if the stone was talking to him. Bending closer he listened to the gentle whisper inside his ears, wondering if the sound could really be coming from the stone.

Convinced that the pebble was no ordinary find and determined not to walk away, Dylan looked around for something that he could use to protect his hands from the heat. He found nothing. The paving was clear. The local sweeper had done his job well. Then Dylan remembered the newspaper that he had just purchased. Even though the stone was hot, it was not glowing. With luck, the newspaper would not burn when he attempted to pick it up.

Unrolling his purchase until it was completely flat, Dylan placed it under one end of the stone. Using his foot as a brake at the other end to prevent it from rolling away, he scooped the object from the floor. As the stone lay trapped on top of the print the paper began to discolour, thankfully it did not catch fire. Either the stone had cooled since his first attempt to pick it up, or the heat was not as intense as he'd first thought.

With the stone now lying flat on the surface of the top page, Dylan began rolling the paper tightly around it, twisting both ends to keep it from falling out. Once it was safely tucked away, he strode the two blocks to his apartment. Turning the key in the lock, he opened the front door and made his way into the narrow hallway careful not to open the door too wide. Although he'd been gone only a short amount of time his Jack Russell terrier Buttons, as expected was waiting behind the door, her tail wagging ferociously.

"Hello girl," Dylan laughed as she jumped up excitedly. "You miss me, eh? You do know I've only been gone fifteen minutes?" Buttons didn't seem to care. She followed Dylan through the hallway and into the kitchen wagging her tail so hard it looked as if it might fall off. Placing the newspaper onto the wooden unit beside the sink, Dylan dropped to his knees and petted her, marvelling at how pleased she always was to see him.

The dog was his best friend. She was far better than any human he'd ever known. Her love was unconditional, unlike the family that had once shared his life. As he'd grown up had quickly come to realise that most people were vile and untrustworthy. It seemed that everybody was out for something, never bothered by the chaos that they left in their wake. They created war and famine and destroyed the planet that sheltered them, oblivious to the damage that they caused.

When Dylan turned on the tv set it was always the same images flashing on the screen. He'd hang his head in shame dumbfounded by man's barbaric nature. Turning away in disgust one evening after yet another horrific news report, he'd finally decided that it was time to disassociate himself from the rest of his kind. He didn't have a girlfriend, and he didn't care so living alone was easy. If he'd gotten the chance he'd have moved to some uninhabited island and ceased contact with all human beings completely.

Pushing himself up from the floor and trying not to step on his dog as she ran between his feet, Dylan carefully unrolled the newspaper to expose the stone lying inside. Sticking out his finger he tentatively touched the surface, testing the object's heat, prepared to whip his finger away quickly if it was still too hot to touch. He needn't have worried. The surface had completely cooled.

Picking the stone up and turning it over in his hands, Dylan noticed the inscription carved into the back. Putting on his reading glasses he read it aloud, "Venit Lumen De Chao. Wonder what it means?" he said looking down at his dog. "Any idea girl?" Buttons cocked her head and looked up at him, her ears pricked, her body alert. "Yeah, that's what I thought," Dylan laughed.

Making his way out of the kitchen with the stone still clasped tightly in his right hand, Dylan headed to the front room and clicked on his computer. Once the machine had warmed up and the screen had fully illuminated, he typed the inscription from the stone into his search engine. "It's Latin," he muttered looking back down at his dog. "It means, From Chaos Comes Light. Cool huh? I wonder who wrote it."

Buttons wagged her tail as if understanding every word, causing Dylan to break into laughter. "You are crazy, do you know that?" he grinned, shaking his head, and turning off the computer. Come on girl, I think we deserve a break, don't you?" he said, grabbing her harness and lead and saddling her up.

Leaving the stone on the table. He made his way out of the flat then headed back down to the beach. For the next hour, he played on the seafront, throwing sticks, and letting buttons run free, taking advantage of the new relaxed winter guidelines. Once he was sure he'd tied the dog out, he made his way back home.

When Dylan had thoroughly cleaned the young dog and washed out all the seawater from her fur, he emptied a tin of dog food into her bowl and returned to the front room trying to decide what to do with his recent find. It would certainly make a great ornament that was for sure.

He just needed to figure out where to put it.

As he made his way towards the computer table he stopped. "What the hell?" he muttered. The stone was no longer there. Wondering if he was going mad, he quickly began checking each room, deciding that he must have moved the stone and placed it somewhere else before he left. He found it in his bedroom. The stone was lying on his pillow and had burned a small dark hole into the material.

"What the hell is going on here?" He mumbled looking down at the shiny black object warily. Picking it up from the pillow, confused as to how it had gotten there, he staggered back and fell against the wall. He suddenly felt giddy. His head began to hurt. The pain was gradual at first, but it built in intensity until his whole head had become one dull throbbing ache. Feeling a little nauseous, he stumbled into the kitchen and reached for the medicine cabinet.

He was starting to feel dizzy. The room was beginning to spin. As he poured a glass of water from the tap, his hands began to shake. Somehow, he managed to pop out a couple of tablets from the foil. As he put them into his mouth and lifted the glass to his lips, bile rose in his throat.

Hanging his head over the washing-up bowl, he threw up the remains of his dinner. Again, and again, he reached, his body racked by spasms as the contents of his stomach were disgorged into the sink. Finally, when there was nothing left inside of him, he managed to stagger out of the kitchen and into the toilet.

Carrying the bowl awkwardly in his hands, he pushed open the toilet door and flushed the contents down the pan. Blinking away tears he stretched out his hand to reach for the toilet roll. The dizziness returned. As the room began to spin again, Dylan dropped to the floor, the world turning dark as he slipped into unconsciousness.

***

When he opened his eyes, Dylan was no longer in his apartment. Instead, he was lying on the cold surface of a cave floor. His dog Buttons was lying on her belly beside him, completely still, her ears bent forward, alert and staring ahead. As Dylan lifted his body to stand the dog looked up at him. She licked his hand but didn't move.

Dylan's head felt heavy He felt as if he'd awoken from a deep slumber. Staring into the gloom he saw that he wasn't alone. In front of him were a small group of people, four men, and five women. They were sitting in a tight circle with an empty space amongst them smiling at him as if they'd been waiting for him to wake. On the ground in front of each person was a black stone similar to the one he'd found by the beach.

What the hell was going on? What did it all mean? Confused as he was, he knew that he had no reason to be scared, something within him, a voice maybe was telling him that this was ok, that this was part of a process, that his being here had always been intended.

"You feel it don't you?" The girl sitting opposite him asked, as he joined the group and took his place in the circle. She was roughly the same age as Dylan maybe thirty or so. She was wearing a red dress only a few shades deeper than her hair. Her face was covered with freckles.

As he sat down the girl watched him intently, clearly amused by his struggle to make himself comfortable on the hard surface. She waited for him to speak, never averting her eyes for a moment, needing to know if he felt the same connection. Ridiculously, Dylan did. It was as if something inside him was shouting at him, telling him that this was his destiny, that his life had always been leading to this point, that fate had prepared him for this very moment.

"I do feel something," he managed to blurt out. "I don't understand it, but I know it's real. I can't pretend I have a clue as to what's happening to me or how I got here, but it's as if I know you as if I've always known you. How can that be?

"Who cares," a large man sitting a few feet away replied. "You're here. That's all that matters right?" The guy was a giant. Even though he was sat cross-legged like the rest of the group, he towered above everyone around him. Despite his intimidating bulk, he had a soft friendly face. Like the others sitting close by, he looked completely at peace with himself.

Dylan studied the rest of the circle wondering what they had in common. They were all probably somewhere between twenty and fifty years old. Each man and woman seemed to be facing someone in their age group. What had brought them all to the cave, what had made them come to this place? He didn't know. In the deep hypnotic gloom, it didn't seem to matter.

As he looked back down at the floor, all the stones began to glow. They turned quickly from black to bright red, then to white. The light intensified, lighting the cave as if powered by ten immensely powerful torches.

"IT'S TIME, IT'S TIME," the group began to chant. They linked hands and began to rock back and forth. Dylan joined them. He couldn't understand what was making him do it, just that he couldn't stop. He closed his eyes and let the energy that was building inside him take him completely. As he rocked gently from side to side, he felt the electricity rising from the floor and coursing through his body using him as a conduit. It cracked and popped, spilling out of every pore. Tears formed in his eyes. They were tears of joy. He chanted louder his voice echoing and bouncing off the walls of the cave, as he gave in to the euphoria building in his heart.

The ten stones had begun to vibrate. Sparks shot out, connecting and linking them all together. The light formed in the centre of the circle rising above the group's heads, building into a concentrated ball of energy. A huge wall of light shot up through the ceiling of the cave and out into the beyond.

"IT'S TIME, IT'S TIME," the group continued to chant.

Above the cave, the ground began to rumble. The rumbling grew louder until it sounded like thunder. Fault lines appeared in the earth. They snaked out in every direction, across the fields toward the towns and the cities and the rural hamlets, building in strength, building in power. In the streets, the ground began to crack and break. Cars and buses and lorries were sucked into the giant fissures that opened in the earth. Gas lines and water mains burst open, causing explosions that rocked the streets, creating huge walls of fire. Buildings crumbled and fell, bricks and glass crashing down onto pedestrians trapped beneath. Flames licked at the concrete turning it black as terrified men, women, and children ran for cover, desperate to get away.

The ground continued to rumble. Buildings that had stood for hundreds of years bent and broke and crumbled into the soil, reduced to ruins, bleeding stains upon the vast molten fabric of the earth. There was no escape, nowhere to run.

In the sky too, nobody was safe. Huge winds built and tore across the land, some travelling at close to two hundred miles per hour. Black clouds swirled in the sky as the thunder roared. Lightning shot from the heavens, striking the earth. Planes were buffeted by the powerful winds or struck by the lightning that tore them from the sky. Plane after plane plummeted into the ground, their occupants killed by the impact, or by the huge fires that raged in the infernos below.

And still, the earth trembled. The sound grew to a cacophony, splitting the air with an angry roar. Those human beings not yet dead, those still trying to run, were trapped by the explosions that rocked the city. Others were struck by the many power cables that bounced across the roads. The ground cracked and split, opening itself up, a huge gaping wound exposing the hell that lay beneath.

In the seas off the coasts, the winds turned the waves into huge battering rams that smashed and tore at the sides of the vessels that sailed upon them. The waves were huge. They ripped at the ship's hulls, dragging the sailors and the passengers down into a watery grave. Those that didn't drown were torn apart by the hungry sharks circling below.

Across the planet, the same thing was happening, huge swathes of land falling to the powerful energy boiling within the earth. Even the leaders of great nations were not immune. As they ran to their bunkers, they began to realise that nowhere was safe, that there was nowhere left to hide. Rain pummelled the ground spilling across the broken streets, filling the sewers, and over-loading the drains. Huge rivers of water and mud rushed from the hills causing mudslides that added to the mayhem and the chaos, as the ground cracked and bubbled and gave way below. Towns and cities were sucked into the earth as a civilisation that had considered itself invincible was lost forever.

Slowly, the tremors began to subside, and the ground was still again. Nothing was left of what had once been. Man was gone, his great achievements reduced to ash and rubble, his time as a great ruler at an end.

***

In a small cave somewhere in the dark throats of England, the group that had unleashed chaos upon the cities above had ceased chanting. They lay on their sides their eyes closed, resting like fallen dominoes, the last of their energy taken from their still bodies. They had done their job; they had done what was required and now they could rest. They didn't know it yet, nor would they for many days, but they were not the only survivors of Earth's mighty storm. Small pockets of humanity, groups like theirs lay scattered across many continents, locked away, the last men and women of earth.

***

The cave was eerily silent, the small group's breathing the only indicator that the ten men and women that lay upon the floor were not yet dead. It stayed that way for many hours, a cold damp hub housing the small, fragile human seeds that heralded the start of a brave new world.

Dylan was the first to wake quickly followed by the others. Pushing themselves up from the floor, they resumed their positions, quickly grabbing each other's hands. Sitting upright they waited in silence wondering what was to come.

As if responding to something inside her head, a command that only she could hear, the redhead closed her eyes.

"Our mother, the Earth has awoken," she said, her voice softer than before. "She has seen what her world has become, and it has angered her. Today she has taken back that which was lost. She has given the world new light and ripped the darkness away. From this moment the Earth will live again. It will begin to heal. The disease called man will no longer exist. We are the last children of Earth, and she will watch over us. If we are unworthy, she will know, and we will join the rest of our kind. This is our fate; these are her words.

"Why did the mother choose you to speak?" A blonde lady sitting next to the redhead asked as she opened her eyes. "Why not one of us?"

A man sitting next to the giant nodded his head in agreement. "Yes, what makes you so special?" he asked.

The redhead shook her head and let out a big sigh. "Have you learned nothing?" she replied. "We are here, and we are safe, why can we not be grateful for what she has given us? Why must we question her will? The mother knows everything. If we harbour doubt, she will find us and she will be angry."

The rest of the group were watching in silence. Each of them still, each of them waiting, listening, feeling the power of the earth coursing through their bodies. It was time to be judged. Something amazing was about to happen, something beautiful.

Like the rest of the group, Dylan could feel the earth flowing through his body. Her energy felt magical. It coursed through him filling every pore. As he closed his eyes and listened, he thought he could hear the mother's voice in his head talking to him. The voice was soft and comforting. It was almost as if it were talking to him alone. Unlike the rest of the group, he'd refused to open his eyes, scared that if he did the feeling would leave him and go away. The voice inside his head was pure. I was the most beautiful thing he'd ever known. He felt that he would explode with joy. He felt warm. He felt safe. He wondered if the rest of the group were feeling it too.

The stones grew bright again as the voice finally vanished from Dylan's head. As the stones illuminated the cave, the group reluctantly got to their feet. "It's time to leave," the redhead said, pointing toward the exit.

The group paired off into two's and headed toward the lights, that now floated in the air like tiny beacons. As the blonde girl that had spoken earlier reached the exit, she and her partner's bodies went limp. They dropped to the floor, their lives extinguished, like the two stones that clanked and turned grey, turning to ash beside them.

The rest of the group stopped, suddenly afraid, no longer wishing to leave the cave.

"You heard our mother's words," the redhead said, urging them forward. "The Earth knows you know. If your heart is clean, you will leave this place alive. You need only fear if you harbour darkness within you."

The 2nd pair shuffled forward nervously. They reached the exit the lights remaining bright above their heads. Once they'd moved through the small crevice that led the way out, the next couple followed. They never made it. They fell like the first couple that had tried to leave, their stones dropping beside them where they lay.

The process was repeated until finally only Dylan and the redhead remained.

"I guess it's our turn," Dylan said nervously, looking down at the four bodies that lay cold in the dirt. "Whether I make it or not, it would be good to know your name before I depart this place."

"You have no reason to be afraid Dylan, "the redhead replied. "Of everyone in here today yours is the purest heart. I felt it when you arrived. It's why I hoped I'd be chosen to pair with you. My name is Angelica, but I'm sure that doesn't matter. When we leave here, we can be whoever we want."

Dylan didn't know how Angelica knew his name, nor did he care. He looked down at his dog who was waiting patiently at his feet. "You ready girl?" he said stepping toward the cave exit with Angelica holding tightly onto his arm.

The girl was right, Dylan made it through without incident. Soon he and Angelica were stepping out of the cave and into bright sunlight. Ahead of them, the other four survivors were waiting. They stood next to a thick mass of bushes and small trees that had hidden the entrance to the cave from the world beyond.

"I've taken a look ahead," the large man who had spoken to Dylan when he'd first arrived said. He was even bigger standing than Dylan had imagined. He towered over his partner like a giant. "There are fields on the other side of these bushes, but I have to warn you, stuff has happened whilst we have been inside. You might want to prepare yourself for what you are about to see."

Dylan nodded. He followed the small group as they turned and made their way through the thicket. As the big guy had indicated there were fields on the other side of the bushes. In one corner of the field, crumpled in the mud, part of a plane's burnt-out cockpit lay where it had come to rest. In the distance, close to the horizon, Dylan could see plumes of black smoke rising into the sky where towns had once stood.

"Do you hear that?" Angelica asked, tilting her head sideways.

"Hear what?" Dylan asked.

"The silence," Angelica replied. She grabbed his hand. "Listen. We are completely alone. Everyone's gone. The mother spoke the truth, there are no other humans left here."

Maybe ten to fifteen feet away was a herd of deer. They eyed the small dog and the strangers standing silently amongst them but did not attempt to move They were not skittish. It was as if they knew that something had changed.

"They are not scared of us," Dylan mouthed.

"It's because they know," the redhead replied. "The world has changed. The evil has gone from this place. There is no more darkness, no more hate." She was grinning from ear to ear.

Dylan smiled back at her. Something was different. He could sense it. The feeling that he'd had inside the cave was still there. For the first time in his life, he felt truly at peace. The Earth had chosen him. The old order was gone. He was part of something bigger now, something wonderful, something he could never truly explain.

"Is this heaven?" he asked, staring at the girl, then down at his dog.

"Maybe it is," the redhead replied. She looked up at the sky, watching a flock of birds that were flying overhead. "We are the new Adam's and the new Eve's. Come, we have work to do," she said, leading him away.

Ahead Buttons ran and played. She frolicked in the warm soothing rays of a new dawn and Dylan was happier than he'd ever known he could be.

SECRETS

The old lady at the top of Barrow hill had always lived alone. With only a black cat for company, she'd repeatedly shunned any attempt by her neighbours to make her acquaintance. When the villagers met in the streets below, they lowered their voices and whispered to one another, scared that she might hear their mocking words. Why did she refuse to be part of their community, they asked. What secrets was she was hiding from the world? As they gossiped amongst themselves, one fact soon became clear, nobody, not even the older folk could remember the day that Mrs. Baker had arrived. It was as if she'd always been there, a stranger with no past.

***

Yvonne made her way up the short incline that led to number 1 Barrow Hill and stopped outside the gate. Catching her breath, she quietly studied the old lady a few feet away pottering amongst the flower beds. Mrs. Baker was old, much older than Yvonne had been given reason to believe. The old girl must be in her mid to late eighties at least she thought, staring at the mass of wrinkles on her head. The poor dear was likely to keel over very soon and take her last breath. Perhaps it had been a wasted trip. She was certainly starting to think so.

Looking past Mrs. Baker's shoulder toward the house perched neatly at the end of the small gravel path, Yvonne searched for anything that looked out of place, hoping that she could find something that might lend substance to the rumours that she'd heard about the property. Unfortunately, just like the old lady, the house was completely unremarkable. It was dull and boring like all the other buildings in the village below, just a modest two-level building, with neat little edges and a nineteen seventies pebbledash front facia.

Upon hearing Yvonne's approach, the old lady had stopped working. She was looking up from her flowers and observing Yvonne with cold unwavering eyes. Her pupils looked like that of a shark, deep black pools that held no light to shine upon whatever secrets lay in the dark murky pit beyond.

"Hi, my name is Yvonne Braithwaite," Yvonne said stepping toward the gate and introducing herself. "I'm a reporter for a small local paper."

"And you are telling me this priceless piece of information because?" Mrs. Baker replied sarcastically. Pushing herself up from the mud, she wiped her hands on her dress and walked over to the gate, stopping just inches from the reporter.

Yvonne was shocked by how quickly the old woman had managed to cover the distance. For someone of her age, she was incredibly sprightly. When she'd been bent over amongst the flower beds, she'd looked like an old hag, but now, standing erect, it was as if her body had been completely transformed. Her back was straight, not hunched over like so many other women of her years. She looked twenty years younger. It was as if Yvonne was staring at a different person.

"So, what is this all about?" Mrs. Baker asked. "Why are you here? I'm a very busy woman. Please do get the point of your visit."

"I'm sorry," Yvonne replied trying not to laugh at the old lady's blunt tone, "My boss has sent me to interview you. It appears that one or two people around here have been talking about you."

"Yes, they think I'm a witch," Mrs. Baker Replied. "Their own lives must be so terribly boring don't you think? But what about you dear? Do you believe I'm a witch?"

Leaning over the gate, she grabbed Yvonne by both of her hands. "Ah I'm sensing something," she said, gripping Yvonne hard, refusing to let go. "You are hiding something aren't you? You are not here for my story. You are here because you want something from me."

"What would make you say that? I'm a reporter, I go where I am sent."

"I think not," Mrs. Baker replied. "You came here because you had to. I'm the thing you've been searching for your whole life. Yes, you are a reporter, but your paper is just a front. You want so badly for the rumours about me to be true, don't you? I can feel your desperation pouring out of you like a seeping wound. You want me to be a witch you are positively counting on it. Does your boss even know you are here girly? I bet he doesn't."

Yvonne's eyes widened. For a moment she was stuck for words.

"Oh, for God's sake close your mouth," Mrs. Baker tutted. "You look like a fish dear. It is quite unbecoming.

"Ok, you rumbled me," Yvonne muttered. "I did want to find you. I have always believed that you existed, I just needed to prove it. Now that I have finally found you, what happens next? Will you let me come in or not?"

"Well, I suppose since you've come all this way, it would be rude to send you home, wouldn't it?" Mrs. Baker replied. "I don't usually take visitors, but you intrigue me, dear. Anyway, you can't interview me on the doorstep, can you? What would my feckless neighbours think then?" She opened the gate and beckoned Yvonne to follow.

Leading the young girl up the garden path,

she produced a key from a torn pocket on her dress and opened the front door to her house. The door creaked loudly as the couple made their way inside. Passing a rather untidy front room, Mrs. Baker led Yvonne through to the kitchen and instructed her to sit at the wooden table that occupied a large space in the centre of the floor. "Tea?" she asked, making her way over to the stove a few feet away and lighting one of four gas rings on which an old worn kettle sat.

"Thank you," Yvonne replied. She watched as Mrs. Baker prepared two cups and placed them on the table, marvelling at the ease with which the old lady's withered body moved.

"Right, now where were we?" Mrs. Baker said, taking a seat opposite her guest and pouring boiling water into the teapot. "Ah yes, you were about to tell me what you are doing here weren't you."

"I know that I should be answering your question," Yvonne said, pouring the tea into her cup and helping herself to sugar. "But since you seem to be able to read me like a book, I have a feeling there isn't much I can tell you that you don't already know. You on the other hand have much to tell. There is much more to you than

I first believed. Maybe what you said outside is true, maybe you are the one I've been searching for all this time."

Mrs. Baker threw her head back and laughed. "You possess a little power of your own don't you girl? I sensed it the moment you approached my gate. Your power though is very tame. Oh, you can do nice little tricks, things that probably amaze your friends at parties, but it bothers you that you can't do more. Does it upset you, dear? Do you feel it ripping you apart? Every time you have to perform like some pathetic puppy, you feel like a piece of you has been stripped away. Tell me I'm wrong."

Yvonne shook her head. "No. You are right. What else do you see?"

"One day, not so long ago I'd imagine, you did something that changed you," Mrs. Baker replied. "It changed you in ways that you could never come back from. You found something that you hadn't expected to find didn't you? After that, you didn't want to let it go. You felt it bubbling inside you like a volcano. The feeling burnt and tore through every sinew in your body, and you liked. When it disappeared, you were left empty and baron. Now that you've tasted it, now that you've experienced true magic, you want it for keeps."

"Right again."

"When did this thing happen dear? Tell me your tale."

"I joined a coven," Yvonne almost whispered. "I met a girl who called herself Davinia. The coven was just a game to most of the others there. Nobody took it seriously. It was just a bunch of bored teenagers and middle-aged housewives who'd watched one too many tv shows and were searching for something to perk up their rather dull lives. Davinia, she was different, she believed. We became close. We wanted the same things. We understood one another."

"So, what happened?"

"Just over a year ago, after one too many drinks, the two of us performed a séance. We called something dark. That night, for a brief moment we rose beyond the spiritual plains. Whilst we were free of our bodies something entered us. It invaded our sleeping minds and learned our deepest secrets. For a short time after we could perform magic tricks the like of which we never knew we were capable of, but it didn't last. We kept going back for more. We'd become addicted to whatever this thing was that had taken us. The problem was, there was a price to pay, we just didn't know. I don't know who or what we called, but we soon realised that it wasn't clean, it had come from somewhere dark, and we had no idea how to push it back. I didn't realise it until it was too late, but the power that we had invited wanted a life. Eventually, it came to take one of us. That day Davinia's parents found her in her room. She was lying on her bed. She never woke again."

"And you still haven't learned the lesson you were taught that night, have you? Your friend died for you, but still, you come to me hoping that I can give you something that you don't deserve to possess."

"I need it," Yvonne snarled. "I know I ask a lot of you, but I can't live this lie anymore. My eyes have seen a different world now. How can I ever go back to what I was before having seen the things I've seen?" I don't know if you're a witch but if you are, you have to help me."

"You show me yours; I'll show you mine," Mrs. Baker cackled.

"I'm sorry?" Yvonne replied.

"Your power girl. Show me what you can do.

Let me know if you are worthy. If I decide that I want to help you, I'll let you know."

"Ok," Yvonne agreed.

Closing her eyes, she focused her mind and concentrated hard on the table in front of her. Slowly it rose into the air until the bottom of the legs were just inches from the two ladies' heads. Yvonne allowed the table to hover for a moment longer then dropped it gently to the floor.

"A party trick," Mrs. Baker said, clearly unimpressed. "Nothing more."

"So, show me what you can do," Yvonne responded angrily."

Mrs. Baker clicked her fingers. The table disappeared. Yvonne stared at the space in which it had sat only seconds before. "Where has it gone?" she asked.

Mrs. Baker indicated toward the front of the house. "Go through child, see for yourself."

Yvonne walked to the door and peered around the corner. The table was sitting upside down on the front room carpet with all of the other furniture from the room stacked on top, balancing at precarious angles. Yvonne looked back at the old lady and clapped her hands.

"Do you believe me now?" Mrs. Baker

asked.

"Yes, I do," Yvonne said in awe.

Mrs. Baker clicked her fingers. The Table was suddenly back in front of her. "Drink your tea dear, it's getting cold," she said picking up her cup and lifting it to her mouth.

"So have you decided whether you are going to help me?" Yvonne asked.

"No not yet," Mrs. Baker replied. "There is a darkness in you. I fear that if you ever possess the power that you ask for, you might use it to wreak havoc upon the world. How can I know that you would not use your gift in such a way?"

"You don't," Yvonne replied, "But you'll help me just the same."

"And why would that be my dear?"

"I have a friend who works for the national papers, he owes me a favour. If I walk away from here without getting what I came for, I'll call him. I'll tell him your secret. I'll make sure he ruins you. The press will descend on you in droves, they'll hound you until you are broken and screaming on the tiles. You'll never know peace again."

Mrs. Baker's face turned red. She turned her palms upside down and whispered an incantation. A cold wind blew through the kitchen ripping the doors wide open. Yvonne's body rose to the ceiling. She jerked and writhed, struggling to breathe, clawing at the air as her lungs searched for precious oxygen.

"I could kill you right now if I wanted to," Mrs. Baker snapped. "What would your pathetic friends do then? Do you seriously believe they could hurt me? Do you think I'm scared of you little girl? Don't you dare to ever presume to threaten me in my home!"

As Yvonne's eyes began to bulge and she came perilously close to death, the old lady let her go. Yvonne dropped back into her seat swallowing life-saving air, thankful to be alive. "I'm sorry," she croaked, "I shouldn't have tested you; it was wrong."

Mrs. Baker was quiet for a moment. "You have been punished enough," she decided. "You know that what you did was wrong, you are sorry. Let us talk of it no more."

Taking a sip of her tea, she studied at the younger woman for cy a moment deep in thought. "You want this badly, don't you?" she said putting the cup back down. "You want it so much that you were prepared to risk your life for it."

Yvonne nodded.

"The kind of power you crave isn't easy to obtain. You must know that. There is only one way that I know of to pass it onto you. Such a gift comes with a heavy price. Are you willing to do what is necessary? Are you happy to accept the cost?"

Yvonne nodded her head. "Does that mean you've decided to help me?" she inquired, still unsure if the old lady intended to help her.

Mrs. Baker slipped out of her chair. "Follow me," she said, turning and leading Yvonne through the house and upstairs to one of the back bedrooms. She stopped beside the bed and pointed to a painting on the wall.

"It's a great picture," Yvonne said staring at the lady in the oil painting. "Who is she?"

"The woman's name is Mary Cheverell," Mrs. Baker replied. "She was burnt at the stake in the late sixteenth century, accused of witchcraft. Unlike many other unfortunate women who died during that time, Mary did possess great power. Her power was I'm told, even greater than mine."

"But she's dead, why are you showing this to me?"

"Touch it," Mrs. Baker replied. Once you

do, you'll understand."

Yvonne stepped around the bed and let her fingers brush over the picture. She pulled her hand away quickly a shocked but excited look on her face.

"You felt it?" Mrs. Baker asked

"Yes," Yvonne replied. "My arm tingled like a bolt of electricity had entered it. It came from the painting didn't it."

"Mary knew that she was going to die," Mrs. Baker explained. "Somebody had learned of her secret and told the church. Knowing that her time was short, she hid away and had this painting commissioned. Casting a spell, Mary passed all of her most powerful magic into the picture, hoping that if she were ever reborn, she'd be able to take it back and exact her revenge upon the world. It has been hidden inside that painting ever since. Mary is never coming back of course. Her body was burnt to ashes, her brief but eventful life scattered to the four corners by the wind. That picture and what lies inside is all that remains of her now."

"And you know how to release the magic?" Yvonne gasped excitedly. "Please, I beg you, if you do, you have to pass it on to me."

40

"Are you sure you want this girly?" Mrs. Baker asked. "The magic you seek is dark, much darker than you can ever imagine. If you take it, there will be consequences, you must be prepared for that. You must be ready to accept whatever comes to you because of your stealing Mary's gift."

"I'm ready," Yvonne replied, "Mary can't hurt me. She's dead. I'm not stealing from her. Her magic is a gift from one witch to another."

"Ok," Mrs. Baker sighed, "So be it. I've warned you of the risks and you still wish to proceed. I will do what you ask, but on your head be it."

"What do we need to do?" Yvonne asked. "I want to begin immediately."

"I will need to paint your portrait and lay it beside Mary's. Then I will perform a small ritual. The ritual that I will perform will bind the pictures together. Once done we will be able to take the power from her picture and transfer it to your painting. Afterward, we'll burn her portrait trapping the magic in your picture. The power will then be there for you to take. It will live inside you forever. Are you sure this is what you want?"

"It is," Yvonne replied.

"To paint your portrait, you will need to stay at this house. Ring your mother or whoever it is that you live with, let them know that you are safe, tell them you'll be gone for a while."

***For the next few days, Yvonne posed, and Mrs. Baker painted. They stopped only to eat, drink and sleep. By the end of the fourth day, the picture was finished.

Yvonne was sitting alone in the kitchen eating a jam scone when Mrs. Baker called her up to the bedroom. "The painting is dry. Come take a look, tell me what you think?"

Yvonne studied her likeness. The picture was amazing. Mrs. Baker had captured every detail perfectly. Her golden hair, her emerald, green eyes. The old lady was a very talented artist.

"You have many depths," Yvonne said turning her head and looking over at her. It's almost as if these two paintings were done by the same hand."

"They are. How else do you think I came to possess Mary's Painting?" Mrs. Baker winked.

Yvonne was genuinely shocked. "You painted them both?" she stammered. "But that would mean that you are hundreds of years old. How is that even possible?"

Mrs. Baker didn't answer. "This is your last chance," she said staring at the girl with cold unwavering eyes. "You can still back out. It's not too late. You can still walk away from this."

"Hell no," Yvonne replied. "Squander a chance like this? I can't. I won't go back to what I was. I'm sick of being a nobody. Let's start the ritual right away. I don't want to wait a moment longer."

"So be it," Mrs. Baker sighed. She pulled a vial containing a green liquid from her dress pocket. "Drink this then lie on the bed."

"What is it?" Yvonne asked.

"Eye of newt, frogs' tail, the usual," Mrs. Baker teased.

"Guess I asked for that," Yvonne laughed.

"It's a little something to help you to relax," Mrs. Baker explained. When I begin my spell, I'll need you to have a completely clear head. You must be in a trance-like state if this is to work. Your mind must be devoid of thought or emotion so that yours and Mary's essence can unfold and evolve."

Ok," Yvonne replied. Drinking the vial as instructed she lay down on the bed and made herself comfortable.

As she waited for the potion to work, Mrs. Baker placed the paintings on either side of her body. Then she covered Yvonne's stomach and breast in flower petals. Once enough petals were in place, she began scattering an assortment of herbs, leaves, and one or two other bits and pieces Yvonne didn't recognise across the sheets. The old lady then lit candles around the bed and begun to chant.

Yvonne felt her mind begin to drift. Her body felt light as if it were being carried away on a gentle breeze. Although she could still hear Mrs. Baker chanting, her voice no longer seemed clear. It had gotten slowly quieter, disappearing into the distance as if she were no longer in the room.

Yvonne lay still. She strained her ears. Mrs. Baker's voice had become nothing more than a whisper. For a moment Yvonne was afraid. She stiffened on the bed listening hard, but she could hear nothing at all. It seemed as if the old lady's chanting had ceased completely.

Yvonne suddenly became aware of every change in her skin. It felt different now. Her body felt warm. She was starting to feel uncomfortable. Even in her trance-like state, her mind was confused. She could feel a dark presence entering her. "Her brain couldn't comprehend the change. "Am I not supposed to wake first?" the voice inside her head was yelling.

Although Yvonne's clouded mind was struggling hard to remember the exact conversation, she'd had with Mrs. Baker earlier in the day, she instinctively knew that something wasn't right. She fought against the fog that covered her thoughts, desperate to find the answer that hung like a cloud, hovering just beyond her reach

"The power must be taken once Mary's picture has been burned," she said snapping open her eyes. "The old hag is up to something."

Yvonne's legs were beginning to hurt. She looked down at her feet. She was no longer on the bed. Flames were licking at her skin. She screamed in pain as the fire danced into the air spreading quickly around her legs. She tried to get away, but she was trapped. With horror, she realised that her body had been tied to a wooden stake.

Beyond the fire that was burning fiercely now, Yvonne could see a huge crowd gathered in the square. "Burn witch burn!" they were chanting at her.

A few rows back, standing at the edge of the crowd, dressed in the same black dress as in her portrait was Mary Cheverell. Next to her and holding onto Mary's hand was Mrs. Baker.

As the two women began to walk away, Yvonne could hear Mary whisper. Her words floated through the air above the crowd and into Yvonne's ears.

"Thank you," she said. "Thank you for releasing me."

THE BOY WITH NO FACE

The man who emerged from beneath the dark waters of the Spuyten Duyvil Creek had no memory of who he was or where he'd come from, but something, an outside force maybe, was compelling him to head toward the swing bridge that lay ahead at the tip of the creek where the water met the Hudson. Dressed only in a pair of three-quarter length jeans and nothing else, he should have already succumbed to the freezing temperatures of the chilling December waters, but surprisingly he wasn't cold.

Powering through the creek he eventually reached the bridge and attempted to pull himself up onto the concrete blocks, every muscle in his body straining, as he fought against both the currents below and lack of purchase above. When he finally managed to break free and hoist himself out, he was surprised to see the child sitting next to the track.

The child was young, maybe only ten or eleven years old. He was wrapped up well against the elements in a thick padded coat and gloves. He was wearing a beany hat, but his blonde locks were still visible beneath the rim. As the man got closer, he realised that the boy had no face.

"What happened to you?" The man asked, pulling himself over the edge of the concrete and dripping water onto the tracks.

"Nothing," the boy responded.

"Then where's your face? Why don't you have one?"

"I don't have one because it has not been formed. The future is uncertain, it has not been written yet."

"Sorry, but that makes no sense," the man responded, dropping down beside the boy.

"Why should you? I wouldn't expect you

to. All I need to know is that you are ready. I've been waiting for you; I was beginning to think you weren't going to come, but you are here now."

"Why were you waiting for me?" the man asked. "How do you know who I am? What could you possibly want from me?"

"Your name is Charles Gantz," the boy re-marked, "And I've come to guide you."

"Guide me where?" Gantz replied bitterly. You say you bought me here, but I don't know why. What's going on? My head hurts, it's pound-ing. I have this terrible rage inside of me, it burns like a fire. Can you help me put it out?"

"I think I can," the boy replied jumping from his perch. "Get up. Are you going to sit there feeling sorry for yourself all night or are you going to let me guide you home?"

Gantz got to his feet. "You have no eyes, yet you see me. You have no mouth, yet I hear you speak. What kind of magic is this?" he asked.

"Do I have to explain?" the boy said shaking his head and tutting. "Honestly, who is the kid here? Yes, I see you, Mr. Gantz, why would I not? I have no eyes, but I have a brain. I see from within; my senses are working to do what my eyes can't. Now that I've explained, can we please get out of here? It's way past my bedtime and it is quite cold you know."

Gantz got to his feet. "Where are we going?"

"To put right a wrong. Follow me and I'll help you to remember."

Jumping down from the tracks, the boy headed out toward some lights twinkling in the distance beyond the creek.

"What is that over there?" Charles asked, following the boy's lead.

"That's the Bronx," the boy replied. "Your home, the place you came from before it all happened."

Images began to flash inside Gantz's head. It felt like a series of flash bulbs going off one by one, illuminating some distant memory, some part of his past that he thought he'd erased. "I remember," he said stopping still. "I remember everything. Jack Turner tried to kill me, he took my life and dumped me in the river. The bastard left me for dead, didn't he?"

The boy turned around. "That's right," he replied. "And tonight, you will make him pay for what he did to you. You will make him suffer as you have suffered."

Charles nodded. "I'll make him pay alright."

The two of them walked in silence. Above their heads, it had begun to snow. Although the snow was light, some of the flakes were already beginning to settle. The boy pulled his coat tighter. The pair walked on, their feet crunching quietly on the ground.

Soon they had reached the edge of the city. The boy stopped. "We'll need to keep to the shadows," he whispered. "And we'll try to find you a coat. I don't want you to freeze."

The older man agreed. Snaking ahead, he ducked into an alley with the boy following close behind. Keeping close to the walls and using the shadows that loomed from the many tall buildings towering overhead as cover, they powered on. Even now, in the dead of the night, the city seemed to be teeming with activity. People milled around, sirens wailed, and car horns tooted as the city breathed and shook with life.

Halfway along the alley, Charles came across an old bum lying down amongst some pieces of cardboard. His body was wrapped up in a sleeping bag and he was fighting to keep warm in the doorway of a building, shielding himself from the snow that was falling harder now.

"I need your coat," Charles said stepping

close. The bum looked up at him, concern etched into his eyes. He tried to wriggle from his sleeping bag, but the younger man was too quick. "Give it to me," he commanded."

The bum shook his head and held onto the bag.

"Ah screw this," Gantz mumbled. Before the homeless man had a chance to fight back, he had leaned down and grabbed the unfortunate man by the head. Twisting hard, he snapped the bum's neck. With the vagrant no longer a problem, Gantz pulled him from his sleeping bag and took his clothes.

"Did you have to do that?" the boy said, hugging himself against the cold. "He was just a defenceless old man."

"Guess it was an over-reaction," Gantz apologised. "Are you going to leave me?"

The boy shook his head. "No, but we have to move. We are running out of time."

"Ok, let's go," Charles said looking up at the sky. The snow was falling harder. The temperature had dropped considerably. Throwing on the bum's jacket and shoes, he signalled to the boy that he was ready, and the unlikely pair began moving again.

They moved quietly from one street to another, using the alleyways wherever they could and always keeping close to the walls. Whenever they had to walk into a crowded street or pass a lone pedestrian, the boy kept his head low, making sure that nobody could see his face.

Finally, they reached their goal, an old apartment building in the south of the Bronx, in a particularly poor part of the neighbourhood. The whole area was run down after years of neglect. Even so, it was a place that Gantz had grown up in and the place that he'd called home. Turner had taken it all away when he'd shot him in the face and left him to die.

As Charles Gantz got ready to climb the steps to the front of the building, the boy stopped him. He indicated toward a bin next to the steps.

"What you want me to go through the trash?" Gantz asked, confused.

"No," the boy replied, "Behind it, I've left you something. If you are going to kill him, you want to make sure you do it right. You don't want to fail do you?"

Charles searched behind the bin. He found the revolver, partially covered by snow, next to a pile of old bricks. "Does it work?" he asked, opening the cylinder, and feeling with his fingers for the bullets inside.

"It works," the boy responded. "I oiled it before we met up. It's time for you to use it. Turner is inside your house. He's laughing at you. Are you going to let them get away with that?"

"No," Gantz growled. "I'm not. Is Maria in there with him?"

"Yes. You must make them both pay. It's time to get your revenge."

Gantz hesitated. He was no longer sure. How could his wife help a stone-cold killer like Turner? He'd been convinced that she'd loved him. Had she been faking it all along? Had their marriage been a lie?

"Don't feel sorry for her," the boy said reading his mind. "She knew what he was going to do. She let him hurt you. She could have stopped him, but she didn't."

"No, she wouldn't do that to me," Gantz snapped. "I can't believe that I won't believe that."

"Then go see for yourself. She's probably holding him tight in her arms, enjoying the fact that you are gone and that she'll never have to sleep with you again."

Gantz let out a roar of anger and headed back toward the steps. "How could I have been so wrong about her? I can't believe I never noticed the signs," he growled.

Reaching the top of the steps, he forced the building's entrance door open and began climbing the three flights of stairs to the third floor. The boy kept close, following him, keeping tight, knowing that the end was close at hand, mentally willing Gantz forward.

Gantz stopped outside the apartment door. It was just how he remembered it. The same dirty green paintwork, grubby and old. He wasn't sure how long he'd been gone, but apart from some peeling in one or two places, nothing had changed.

His heart thumping in his chest, he reached out and tried the handle. The door was locked. It didn't matter. There were other ways to get inside. Pulling the revolver out from where he'd tucked it into the back of his waistbelt, he aimed and fired at the lock. The lock disappeared along with half the woodwork around it. Gantz was through the doorway before Turner, or his wife had time to jump from the couch. They were frozen in their seats, staring at him wide-eyed, completely taken by surprise.

Gantz aimed the gun at his wife's head. "Are you happy to see me Maria?" he asked. "I hope you are, coz you are going to die, just like that shit sitting beside you. Did you think I wouldn't come for you, that I'd let you get away with what you did to me?"

Maria Gantz's face had changed. Her expression was one of both confusion and wonder. "Is that really you?" she gasped. "It can't be can it?" she blurted the words out, clearly fighting with herself, wanting to believe what her eyes were telling her, but knowing that what she was seeing couldn't possibly be real.

"You died," she stuttered, "I watched them bury you, I mourned your passing." She tried to get up from the couch, but her strength had deserted her.

"Stay down!" Gantz screamed at her. "I didn't tell you that you could move."

"You won't hurt me," Maria said, sinking back into the leather seat, "You can't. You don't have it in you."

"Don't I?" Gantz spat. "You let Turner shoot me, then you took him as your lover. Why wouldn't I hurt you?"

"That's not true. I would never have betrayed you like that."

"I loved you, Maria," Gantz said raising his gun higher. "How could you have done this to me?"

Maria's eyes were sparkling with excitement. As Gantz pointed the barrel at her face she should have been scared, instead, her body was filled with an inner warmth. "It is you, isn't it?" she whispered. "Even after the nine years you've been gone, I'd know you anywhere." Her hand was over her mouth, she was shaking her head. Tears flowed freely onto her cheeks, memories of the night he'd been taken returning in waves.

"Don't do that," Gantz muttered. He was fighting with himself, unable to watch his wife's tears, torn between shooting her and holding her in his arms. "Please, I beg you, stop," he pleaded.

"Shoot her," the boy ordered. "She's messing with your head. Can't you see what she is doing? She's playing you. You have to kill her; you have to kill her now."

"Why are you doing this?" Maria said wiping tears from her face. "My Charlie would never want to hurt me. If you are my husband, then search inside yourself, know that I could never have done what you accuse me of."

Gantz turned the gun toward Turner.

"I think she's telling the truth," he growled, "But what about you? Why shouldn't I just put a bullet in your head?"

"Hey, take it easy," Turner replied staring uneasily at the gun. You don't have to do this. Whatever it is that you think I've done, you've got this all wrong."

"He's lying," the boy growled. "Kill him."

"The boy tells me you are lying," Gantz snapped. "What do you say to that?"

"What boy? Who the hell are you talking about?" Turner asked. He looked past Gantz's shoulder then turned back. "There's nobody there you nut job, the boy is in your head. He's not real."

"Shut up!" Gantz screamed. "The boy bought me here. He helped me remember. He is watching you right now. Are you calling me a liar?"

"Hey, let's all cool down, shall we?" Turner said softening his tone. "I heard what happened to you, Mr. Gantz. Your wife told me everything. They found you near the river am I right? I guess you must have survived. Maybe they buried the wrong man. Is that what happened? You're angry, you lost everything. I get it. I would be angry too. The bastard that mugged you took your life. He may not have killed you, but he took it anyway."

"Stop it!" Gantz shouted. "I know what you are. You're the man I met that night. I know you. I know that it was you that mugged me."

"Is he telling the truth?" Maria asked, turning to face her partner.

"No," he replied, "you have it all wrong. Please, I've never met your husband before. You have to believe me."

Gantz's hand was trembling. He was rubbing the gun up and down against his cheekbone a few inches from where his eyes, no longer sure what was real. What if Turner was innocent? What if he was telling the truth? He was beginning to doubt the boy. "How do I know you aren't lying to me?" he asked, turning his head, and looking down at the child. "I don't know you. Why do you want me to kill this man so badly? What's in this for you?"

"What do you think is in it for me?" the boy replied. "If you don't know by now, maybe I'm wasting my time here."

"I haven't figured that out," Gantz replied. "But there's something about you. I knew it when I saw you by the river. I felt a connection, I still can't explain it.

"Look inside yourself." The boy muttered. "You know who I am. You've known all along."

As Gantz looked on, the boy's skin began to change. His face rippled and became whole. As Charles looked into his eyes, he found himself staring at his reflection. The boy was Gantz as he had looked when he was a child. "You're me," he gasped, "I get it now."

"Now you see me, you know I speak the truth," the boy said. "Punish him. Let your voice be the last this man ever hears in this world."

Turner was watching Gantz intently. As the would-be killer conversed with the unseen child, he took the opportunity to fumble for the gun he'd tucked down into the crease between the cushions of the couch. "You have it all wrong about me Gantz," he said feeling for the gun with his fingertips and stalling for time. "You know you have to let this thing go. Your wife thought you were dead; you can't blame her for what happened to you. You came back, good for you, but killing either of us won't put things right. Leave the past where it lays. It won't do any good dragging it back up. Whoever shot you is probably long gone. Let it go."

"Shoot him," the boy snarled. "Kill him now. If you don't, he'll finish what he started."

Turner had managed to free the gun. He raised it towards Gantz's head. Gantz saw the movement from the corner of his eye. He pulled his trigger. The bullet exploded through Turner's face, blowing a big hole in the centre of his head, before crashing out through the back of his skull. As Turner dropped off the couch and tumbled onto the floor, something silver rolled from his pocket. It was Charles Gantz's lighter.

"You see that?" the boy said staring at it. "You were carrying that lighter the night you died. Why did Turner have it if it wasn't him that attacked you that night? That lighter belonged to you. He had it all along."

Gantz was shaking. "It's ok, I believe you," he croaked.

The boy turned away; he was staring toward the window. Outside in the street, the night was lit up by blue flashing lights. Police cruisers had converged on the area, alerted to reports of gunshots. Seeing the lights reflected off the walls,

Gantz looked over to where the boy had been standing but he was no longer there. He'd vanished into the air like a ghost.

"What's happening to you..." Gantz heard Maria screeching behind him. "You're fading away. No! Not now, not when I just got you back. Please, please don't leave me again," she wailed.

Gantz stared down at his body. It was rippling and fading in and out of focus. Realising what was happening, he smiled at his wife. "It's ok," he whispered. "I guess it's time for me to go."

Maria started to sob. She stared at Turner's lifeless body then at the lighter lying beside him on the floor. "I'm so sorry," she wailed. I didn't know. You must believe me, Charlie. I was broken. You were dead. I had no reason to go on. I'd lost everything. Turner tricked me; he came to me at my weakest. If I'd known what he'd done to you, I'd never have let him in. He took advantage of my grief. How could I not have known?"

Gantz let his weapon drop from his hand. As Maria sank to her knees, he held her in his arms one last time. "I forgive you," he told her.

As the first officer burst into the room, Gantz's image faltered. A bright light lit up the room. Gantz could feel himself fading fast.

"I love you," Maria yelled, as the light began to rise toward the ceiling, "I always did."

"I know," Gantz replied, as the police led her away.

***Outside the Roosevelt hotel in Manhattan, Michael Frauher was pushing the last of his belongings into the trunk of the yellow cab that sat idling next to the pavement. Michael had had a bad night; in fact, he'd had a bad life. Tonight, though had been the worst of them all. His wife had been sleeping with his best friend. He'd caught them in his hotel room after coming back early from a conference. How long had it been going on he didn't know. His marriage was over, that's all that mattered. As far as he was concerned, the two of them could rot in hell.

As he finished loading the trunk and began opening the back door to jump into the passenger seat, he noticed the boy shuffling on the sidewalk. The boy was blonde around ten or eleven years old and completely alone. What the hell was he doing out in the streets at this God-awful hour for Christ's sake? And with the snow falling. The poor blighter must be freezing. Jeez, what was the world coming to?

"You ok kid?" he asked closing the cab door and stepping back onto the pavement. "Can I help you at all? Can I take you somewhere maybe?"

The boy smiled. "Maybe we can help one another," he replied. He buttoned his coat up against the cold. "Sure, would be good to get out of this snow though sir."

"Yes, it would," Michael responded.

Removing his luggage from the cab's trunk, Michael paid the driver, then turned to face the boy. "I've been staying at the Roosevelt for the last week," he said. "It's a long story but I walked out tonight. My room is paid up for a couple more days. My bitch of a wife is in there right now enjoying my hospitality. Perhaps we should get you in there instead. First, I think we should get you something to eat, after that, we can figure out what to do with her. I'll probably let you have her room until we can find out where you came from and figure how to get you back. Would you like that kid?"

The boy nodded. "She hurt you bad, didn't she?" he sighed. "I can see it in your eyes.

"Yes, she did," Michael replied. "They both did."

"They?"

"Like I said kid, it's a long story."

"She was having an affair with him, wasn't she? You should make them both pay for that. I can help you if you like?"

Michael laughed bitterly. "That would certainly make me feel better I have to admit."

THOMAS BLACK

From the moment Thomas Black had popped out of his mother's belly at St Hue's hospital it was clear that he was different from other children. His parents initially excited by the birth of their only son were soon overcome by an irrational fear. Unable to understand where their child's strange gift had come from, they decided to hide him from the world. Nobody could ever know the dark secret that he held. Thomas would have to be taken away so that the power he possessed could be hidden from preying eyes.

On a bleak winter's night, with the frost's cold fingers pressing down upon a sleeping world, a decision was made. Thomas would be moved. He would live his childhood years in a remote location until such a time came when he could control his curse and walk freely amongst men.

***

James davenport watched appreciatively as Daniella Morgan made her way to his table. She was pretty, much prettier than her photo suggested. Her dark hair and brooding eyes could easily have belonged to a top fashion model. She was dressed in a figure-hugging black dress that showed off every slender curve on her slim, toned body.

"So good to finally meet you," James said politely, as she pulled out the seat opposite him and sat down, "You look amazing."

"Do I?" Daniella replied mischievously. She eyed him across the small space between them through deep hazel brown eyes. "Are you sure?"

James felt himself blush. "I'm sorry," he mumbled. "I'm not very good at this."

"I think you are doing ok," Daniella replied, a big smile on her face. "Every girl likes a compliment."

"Thank you," James said, leaning over and pouring wine into her glass. "It's white, I hope that's ok?"

"Thank you, white is fine."

James stared; he knew it was rude, but he couldn't stop himself. How could somebody so beautiful be sitting at his table? Why would she have been interested in him at all? He had been on several dates in the last couple of years. None had ended well. He guessed that he'd just never found the right girl to make him happy. All the girls he'd dated had been chosen the same way, selected from the internet, picked carefully from a well-known dating site. It was quite an acceptable way to meet and find love nowadays, so he wasn't embarrassed. It was easier than going to some seedy bar, standing around for hours in the hope that somebody might find him attractive. Unfortunately, though the girls always seemed to want something from him. All of them seemed to be angling for a smart car, a new house, or designer jewellery. They all wanted money, something he didn't have.

"Are you ok?" Daniella asked, cutting through his thoughts, and bringing him back into the moment.

"I'm so sorry," James apologised. "Of course, I am, how very rude of me. I was just thinking."

"About what?"

"About you of course."

Daniella smiled. "Good save."

For the next couple of hours, they ate and drank. They talked about their favourite foods, the places they had been, and the people that they had met along the way. The conversation flowed easily with no awkward silences on either side. It was as if they had been destined to meet.

"Why did you pick that photo?" James asked when he'd finished the last mouthful of his dinner. "You look so much better in real life. I'm sure you have better photos than the one you have put up on the internet page..." He stopped himself from going any further, realising how bad the question sounded. "Jeez, that was offensive," he grimaced, "It sounded so much better in my head. What I'm trying to say, rather badly, is that you are stunning Daniella, possibly one of the most beautiful girls I've ever met. Your picture doesn't do you justice."

"Thank you," Daniella replied. "The compliment is nice but unnecessary. Beauty is only skin deep. Yes, you are correct the photo isn't the best one of me, but I don't care. I would like people to get to know me for me. If someone is prepared to make the effort, that surely matters more than what I look like doesn't it? Personality is far more beautiful than an image on a screen. It's what lies inside that makes someone special."

"Yes, I suppose you are right," James agreed.

"As a member of the male species, I'm deeply aware that you are driven by what you see," Daniella said, draining the last dregs from her wine glass. "Men do tend to make decisions based on their groin, but that's what makes us different. As a woman, I see beauty in other forms. I look for kindness, sensitivity, humour. Unfortunately, not everyone possesses such qualities. Not all men are nice. Some are very nasty indeed. At a certain point in my life, I had the great misfortune of meeting such a man. It is a moment that I'd rather forget. Sometimes the past doesn't like to sit quietly in the corner like some tame pet though, does it? It has a horrible tendency to follow you. It waits with rabid teeth biding its time, preparing to jump out of the shadows when you are least expecting it. I don't want to plaster my world with makeup, I'd rather be invisible. I know that my past still lies out there, waiting for a chance to reveal itself to me again. It is hidden from my view right now, festering in its own dark pool of depravity, but I would rather not look into that pool again if I don't have to."

"I see," Michael replied. He stared into Daniella's face and thought he saw something reflected inside her eyes. It was something he didn't like. A feeling of uncertainty suddenly overcame him. Who was she? Why was she staring at him like that? He suddenly felt uncomfortable Was she toying with him? Did she somehow know of his past? She couldn't... How could she? He was being paranoid. He was jumping at shadows that were not there.

"Something really had happened to you, didn't it?" he said, attempting to feign sympathy. "I shouldn't have asked about the picture. I promise I won't ever mention it again. I apologise for having made you drag up hurtful memories."

"It's fine," Daniella replied. "That time is past. It's a distant memory. We were having a nice evening. Please, let's not spoil that. The night is young, let's make the most of it while we can."

"That would be nice, but dinner is nearly over," Michael replied, beginning to relax again. "I hadn't planned any further than that. I didn't know if we'd hit it off. I didn't want to presume."

Daniella laughed. "All of those conversations on the phone, all of those easy hours where I felt like I was talking to an old friend. Are you serious? I don't think I've ever felt so at ease with anybody. Do you want the night to end so soon? It doesn't have to."

Michael had to admit that he didn't. He felt his face flush. He wasn't sure if it was the wine or his embarrassment. Daniella was nice, probably one of the nicest girls he'd ever met. He felt completely comfortable in her presence, yet here he was telling her he wanted to end the night. How stupid could a man be? "So, what now?" he asked, regaining his composure, "Where would you like to go? What would you like to do?"

The mischievous look that had been on Daniella's face when she'd first approached James's table was there again. "We could go back to my place?" she purred.

"Are you sure?" James asked. "It's not too soon? I'd hate for this to be a one-night stand, I like you."

"You are so sweet," Daniella grinned. "I'm not going to eat you I promise. Let's just take it a step at a time. We can have coffee and talk. We can see where it goes from there."

For the 2nd time in less than a minute, James davenport was feeling stupid. "Ok," he laughed. "We'll finish these drinks and grab a taxi."

"Excuse me," a rather embarrassed old gentleman said, approaching the table and interrupting the conversation. "I'm deeply sorry for intruding upon you young lovers, but could you possibly point me in the right direction for the restroom? This is such a large restaurant and I'm afraid I'm totally lost."

"Yes, it's over there," James replied, climbing from his seat, and pointing to the far corner of the building.

"Thank you so much," the man said gratefully.

James watched the stranger navigate his way through the maze of tables scattered across the floor then returned to his date. "Jeez, that will probably be me one day," he laughed.

"Not too soon though eh?" Daniella responded playfully.

"It's ok, I'm not at that point yet," James replied. "I think I can still just about manage to hold my drink without having to run to the toilet."

"Good, then finish your drink and we'll go get that cab."

James nodded. He drained the remaining contents of his glass and signalled the waiter. Once the bill had been settled, the couple left the building and made their way out into the street. They'd only been walking a couple of minutes when James spotted a vacant taxi coming toward them. He waved his arms in the air to hail it down. Opening the back door, he helped Daniella climb in, then slipped in beside her.

Daniella's house wasn't far. It was in an expensive part of Islington, just a fifteen-minute drive from the restaurant. "Wow," James muttered, staring out of the cab window at the posh-looking houses that filled the street, "Maybe I should have let you pay for dinner."

Daniella looked sad for a moment. "I'm not rich," she said, climbing from the taxi and leading him toward the front door. "My mother died seven years ago. This house was left to me. Nice as the house is, I'd rather have my mother back."

"I've done it again haven't I?" Michael replied shaking his head in embarrassment.

"It's ok," Daniella said. "You weren't to know. How could you? It was a tragic accident, just one of those things."

"Even so ..."

Daniella opened the front door. Stepping into the hallway, she switched on the light. "Well, this is it," she said leading him through to the front room. "Make yourself comfortable. I'll go pour us a drink. Is wine, ok? I think it would be a little stupid to start mixing our drinks at this point, but you are quite welcome to have something else if you prefer?"

"Wine is fine," Michael replied.

As Daniella made her way out to the kitchen, Michael sank into the leather couch. Staring at the wooden shelf on the opposite side of the room next to the tv unit, he noticed the photograph in a glass frame between two glass ornaments. The picture was of a young woman. Michael glared at the picture in horror.

"What's going on here?" he muttered, pushing himself up from the couch and making his way over to take a closer look.

With his hand trembling slightly, he took the picture from the shelf and studied it. How the hell had the picture gotten there? What was Daniella doing with it? How did she know the girl? He hoped it was just a coincidence, but the voice inside him told him it wasn't. placing the picture back onto the shelf, fighting to stop his hand from shaking, he turned away. As he made his way back to his seat, he realised that he was beginning to feel a little woozy. He'd only drank a couple of glasses at the restaurant, but the room appeared to be swimming in and out of focus. Staggering back to the couch, he sank into the cushions confused and disorientated.

The minutes ticked past. Daniella seemed to have been gone from the room for a long time, something weird was going on. "Daniella," He called out, trying to get her attention, "What are you up to? Are you coming back or what?"

When he received no reply, his apprehension rose. He attempted to push himself up from the seat, but it was as if he could no longer move couldn't move. His muscles felt tight. It was as if they were starting to seize up. As he struggled to get out of the cushions, the feeling became worse. Within minutes he could no longer move anything but his mouth.

"Daniella what are you playing at?" he mumbled between clenched teeth. "What's going on here?"

He watched the door, frightened by what was happening to his body, wanting it all to stop. He thought he saw movement. "No, no, no it can't be," he cried out as the girl from the photograph entered the room and stopped a few feet away. "Leave me alone, you're not here, I'm imagining you. Get out of my head," he mouthed.

"What's the matter?" Sandra Jones said stepping closer. "You look like you've seen a ghost."

"No, this isn't happening. You're not real. You're dead," James groaned.

"You look frightened," Sandra laughed. "You should be. Did you think you could just kill me and walk away?"

Behind Sandra, standing inside the doorway was the guy from the restaurant. He was holding something in his hand and pointing it at the couch. It looked like a camera of some kind. "Who are you, people?" Michael asked nervously. Where's Daniella?"

"Oh, you want to see her?" Sandra asked. "Did you want to kill her too?"

"No," James replied. "I just want to know what you've done to her."

"What I've done?" Sandra spat. "You murder girls without remorse, yet you dare to point an accusing finger at me."

"What is it you want?" James stammered. "What is this about?"

"Oh, it's quite simple," Sandra explained. "This is about you and the things that you have done. My friend over there wants to record your apology. He wants you to tell him how sorry you are for what you did to me. If you can do what he asks, I promise that I'll call Daniella back. She needs to feel safe before she comes out. You must understand that. She'll need to know that nothing will happen to her. I've told her what you did to me, what you did to all those other girls, and she's deeply concerned. Wouldn't you be?"

James was more frightened than he'd ever been in his life. His heart pounded in his chest. He felt like he might faint. His worst nightmare was playing out before his eyes. "I don't know how you survived," he stammered staring into

Sandra's face," It's impossible. I have to be imagining this. You can't be real, you're dead. I killed you. "I felt my hands crush your throat. I watched the life spark die in your eyes. How can you be here?"

"Then you admit that you took my life?" Sandra asked. "And the other eleven girls... do you admit that you killed them too? Are you are prepared to pay for what you have done?"

"Yes, I killed them. I murdered them all. I took them from their families to satisfy my own dark needs. I'm sorry. I can't take it back. Please, I'll do whatever you say. I wasn't in control. You must forgive me. I'll hand myself in. I'll do whatever you want."

"You get all that?" Sandra asked, turning her head, and glancing over at the old man.

"Yep, full confession, recorded and logged."

"Want to see something amazing?" Sandra asked, turning to face her prisoner, and winking at him."

Michael glared at her, a captive audience, wondering what she was going to do next.

With a sound that was something akin to water pouring over a water feature, Sandra's appearance began to change. Her body began to ripple and bulge. Faces appeared underneath her skin, fighting for space, changing, flowing from one to another. Almost as quickly as one appeared, it was quickly gone. When the rippling finally stopped, and Sandra's body had become still again Daniella stood in her place.

Michael pissed himself. He screamed in terror as Daniella stood grinning at him.

"Yeah, it had the same effect on me the first time I saw that too," the old man said walking over and stopping at Daniella's side. "She's quite something don't you think? You should see her do her Aretha Franklin. It never gets old.

"Who the fuck are you people?" Michael stuttered. He was staring at Daniella, his eyes wide, his mouth opening and closing like a fish.

"The actual name of our unit, not that it matters to you, is Special operations 5," the old man replied. You wouldn't have heard of us of course. Very few people have. We're very new."

"What are you?" Michael davenport muttered. "How can you do that to your body?"

"I guess I'm talented," Daniella replied.

"So, Sandra was never real?" Michael growled.

"Yes, she was very real, just like Daniella.

I'm merely using their shape instead of my own."

"Then who are you?"

"Later," Daniella replied.

"You know you can't arrest me," James said regaining some of his earlier cockiness. "That confession you recorded won't mean shit in court. What you did is entrapment. And you drugged me. Once I get out of here, I'll sue the lot of you."

"Oh, I doubt that" the old man said, reaching up to his face and peeling away the latex mask attached delicately to his skin. "I'm afraid you won't be around long enough to get the chance."

"Ah that feels so much better," he said once the last strips of latex had been removed. "Now where were we?" he asked taking out a tissue and dabbing at the last pieces of sticky residue beneath his eyes. He looked thirty years younger.

"You were about to tell Mr. Davenport why he won't be able to sue you," Daniella responded.

"So I was," the detective grinned. He gazed at Daniella for a moment and shook his head. "Would you mind changing back now?" he pleaded "That whole pretending to be a girl thing is starting to get a little creepy."

Daniella laughed. "Yes of course," she replied. She repeated the process that she'd performed just moments before. When the rippling stopped and her body had become still, a young man with dark hair and piercing brown eyes stood in her place. He was dressed in a blue suit with a pink tie.

"This is Thomas Black," the detective said introducing his colleague. "As you've already guessed, he's a shapeshifter and as far as I know just one of a kind. My name is senior detective John Graham. Both Thomas and I are part of the new unit. It has been created to do what other police units can't."

"What sort of things?" James asked nervously.

"As you are probably aware," Graham began, "We live in a politically correct world. The snowflake generation has to stick their nose into everything. They get upset way too easily. As a result, we must tread carefully. When scum like you get punished too hard, we can't have them crying can we? It looks bad at election time. Unfortunately for you, we've found a way around all that. Our bosses have decided to change the way things are done."

"And that's where we come in," Black interjected.

"Yep, we are completely secret," Graham said jumping back in. We can act with impunity. Practically nobody knows we exist and that's how we like it."

"What's going to happen to me?" Davenport asked. His face had turned pale, he no longer looked confident.

"Well, I guess it would be polite to tell you seeing you don't have much time left in this world," Graham replied.

"You are going to kill me, aren't you?" Davenport said, suddenly aware of his fate. He tried to get up, couldn't. "What did you people give me? Why can't I move?

"Oh that," Graham replied. "Thomas slipped an incapacitate into your drink. It's shut off the signal going to your muscles. Science isn't my thing, but it works, that's all that matters."

Davenport glared at the detective, wishing he could jump up and smash his smug face into the dirt.

"Do you know how much money the government spends on scum like you?" Graham asked. "It's billions son. The hours of police work, the overtime, paying the lawyers, etc. If the police get lucky enough to secure a conviction, the government has to lock you away. They give you a nice cell with tv and have to pay guards to watch over you. That all costs money. It's a drain. It's an expensive business, and people are fed up... So, when the government discovered Mr. Black's rather unusual talents, they got excited. They came up with an exciting idea. Why waste all that public tax money when a better solution is knocking on our door?"

James Davenport looked scared. He knew his time was almost up.

"You look frightened James," Thomas Black said. " I'm glad about that. Scum like you should be."

"My colleague is right," Graham said agreeing with him. "You should be frightened. We're not like other units you see. We have been set up with the sole purpose of removing high-risk targets like you, sex offenders, murders, terror suspects, that sort of thing. Once we get you. We eliminate you. No-fuss, no jails, no more lawyers. It's the perfect solution. The injection that is going to kill you only costs pounds to produce. It will save the government millions."

As Davenport watched on, the detective produced a syringe from his jacket pocket. James tried to struggle but it was useless. "Is it going to hurt?" he mumbled.

"Yes, I'm afraid it is," Graham replied. "I'm not going to sugar-coat it for you. It's going to hurt a lot."

"How does it work?"

"The chemical that enters your bloodstream will cause a fatal heart attack. Not a pleasant death, but you are not a pleasant man," the detective responded. He leaned forward and held the syringe against Sullivan's neck. "Any last words?" he asked.

"Fuck you" Davenport growled.

"Good enough," Graham replied. He pressed down on the syringe until it was empty. Sullivan's body began to spasm. His eyes widened and his face turned white as he writhed in pain. A few seconds later he was completely still. Graham leaned forward and checked for a pulse. There wasn't one. "Time of death, eleven forty-eight," he said looking at his watch.

"Let's get out of here," Thomas Black said heading for the door. Graham followed his lead.

Outside a van was waiting with its engine

running. Graham walked down the path and knocked on the side window.

"Evening Mr. Graham," the driver said, winding down the glass.

"Evening," Graham replied. He handed the agent the keys to the house. "He's all yours," he muttered, "Make sure you do a good job cleaning the place. No traces of what went on here. Am I clear?"

"Crystal," the driver said, watching as the detective ambled away.

SOMEWHERE, NOWHERE

The new house in Belmont Street looked even better than when the agent had handed Bryce Klieser the keys. It stood proud amongst the other properties, its huge white wooden slats gleaming in the warm Ohio sun. Pulling up against the kerb and lining his vehicle with the sold sign just behind the white picket fence, Bryce applied the handbrake and turned off the Toyota's engine. "What do you think?" he asked, twisting his head, and looking over at his wife Rosetta sitting in the passenger seat beside him.

Looking through her side window at the

property, Rosetta couldn't stop herself from grinning. "Isn't it a steal?" she replied shaking her head in disbelief. "How the hell did we get it so cheap?"

"Apparently nobody wants to live here. Can you believe that?" Bryce replied. "The place has been empty for seven years. The agent practically ripped my hand off when I told him I was interested."

"And that didn't worry you?" Rosetta asked, the grin temporarily slipping from her face. "Is there something you are not telling me? There's nothing wrong with the house is there?"

"Aw stop with the negativity will you," Bryce whistled. "There is absolutely nothing wrong I promise. The house is fine. Even better, we don't have to pay rent anymore. We should be rejoicing. As long as we make the payments each month the place is ours, nobody can take it away from us. Come on babe smile. With the mortgage payments being so low, we'll be debt-free in no time.

"Well, I guess it will be good to have our own place," Rosetta agreed. "Let's go take a look inside. You can show me just what we got for our money instead of sitting here biting one another.

How's that sound?"

"It sounds perfect," Bryce grinned.

Rosetta unbuckled her safety belt. "You did a good thing here she purred. "I apologise for my lack of humility. I thank you from the bottom of my heart, I do... Now go get the kettle from the trunk and make me a coffee. I'll go fetch the baby from the back seat and meet you inside."

Bryce didn't need telling twice. Grabbing a few boxes from the back of the vehicle, he made his way up the garden path and headed into the house. His wife would probably be a while he figured. Knowing her as he did, she was probably already outside mentally preparing a jobs list, giving the paintwork a quick once over, looking at what needed to be done once they'd unpacked and settled in. Bryce didn't mind. He wasn't scared of hard work. This house was the first thing he'd ever owned, he'd willingly buckle down and do whatever was needed to be done. His wife and child deserved the best. He was more than happy to give it to them.

The move from Pennsylvania had been hard, but it had also been inevitable. The house he'd rented for nearly five years was never going to be his. When the owner had decided to sell up, Bryce had begun a desperate hunt for another property to rent. Houses were a lot more expensive than he's anticipated and he soon realised that he was heading into trouble. To make matters worse, the factory where he'd been working since leaving school had gone bust. On the spin of a dime, his luck had turned, he was out of work and homeless.

With the factory closing and with no new job on the horizon, Rosetta had decided to lean on family in Ohio for help. Within days, Bryce, his wife, and their new baby Tyler were lodging with Rosetta's mother and father in Washington Street.

The stay turned out to be shorter than either Bryce or Rosetta had anticipated. Within a few months, what had started as a run of bad luck had turned again. Bryce managed to find a new job as a labourer. The work wasn't something he was used to, but he picked it up easily and it paid fairly well. Days after getting the job, he saw the advertisement for the house in Belmont Street. The future was suddenly looking brighter.

Bryce looked up from the kitchen unit as his wife approached. "So, what did you find?" he asked, taking the baby from her arms. "Did

I pass?"

Rosetta picked up her coffee cup and sipped appreciatively at the piping hot drink. "The outside of the house is in remarkably good condition," she said, staring at her husband. "It could do with a lick of paint here and there, but nothing drastic. I guess somebody must have been coming around and doing a little work to keep the place from going under. Whoever it was, I think we should be grateful to them."

"I've had a look around inside. I guess somebody has been busy here too," Bryce grinned. "There's no damp, no obvious faults. The taps all work. There are no cracks, no signs of anything bad that are immediately obvious. The heating even seems to have been serviced recently. We have hot water and electricity. It looks like we have everything we need."

"Well then I guess we should unpack what we have and wait until the rest of our stuff arrives," Rosetta said, unable to contain her excitement.

For the next few days, the couple worked tirelessly, cleaning the house, moving furniture, painting, and putting up shelves. Rosetta's mother and father watched over the baby, making themselves available whenever and wherever they were needed. By the end of the week, everything was gleaming. With the house brought up to a satisfactory standard, the couple moved in properly. They were finally on their own again.

"I have to go back to work tomorrow," Bryce said staring at his wife as she lay in the bed beside him. "They won't allow me any more time off."

"Then I guess we'd best make the most of tonight," Rosetta replied playfully. She leaned over and kissed her husband softly on the mouth.

"Are you trying to seduce me, Rosetta?" Bryce said, a huge smile on his face,

"Yes, I am Mr. Klieser," Rosetta said pulling her husband closer. "Did you want me to stop?"

The pair made love, enjoying each other's bodies, exploring each other as if it were the first time. They writhed and groaned, locked together in a frenzy of arms and legs until finally, their spasms of ecstasy left them happy and exhausted.

Rosetta slept well, but at some time around 2 am, her eyes snapped open. Something had woken her from her sleep. She sat up in the dark and listened. She could hear nothing, just her husband's rhythmic breathing. Even so, something was wrong, she could feel it. Looking over at the baby monitor on the unit beside the bed, Rosetta strained her ears listening for the sounds of crying, but the baby was silent. There were just the usual sounds she'd expect to hear coming from his room, nothing that should have caused her alarm. Maybe it was just a mother's instinct or maybe it was the remnants of a troubled dream, but Rosetta couldn't shake the feeling that her baby was in danger. She decided to go and check on him.

Climbing from the bed, she made her way into the next room and approached Tyler's crib. He looked beautiful, serene even. Even so, Rosetta still couldn't shake the bad feeling bubbling inside her.

Startled by movement out of the corner of her eye, she wheeled around in time to see a figure move across the room. "Die bitch!" the figure whispered. Rosetta's heart thumped in her chest. Had she imagined him? She doubted it. His voice had sounded very real. Picking up her son, frightened by what had just happened, she turned on the light and ran back to her husband.

"Bryce, Bryce," she said shaking him from his sleep. "There's someone in our house."

"What?" Bryce said, sitting up in the bed

suddenly wide awake. "Where? What are you saying? Has someone broke in?"

" I don't know. Something woke me. I went to check on Tyler and I saw someone."

"Who? What did the guy look like?" Bryce said jumping from the bed.

"I'm not sure," Rosetta stammered, "he was there, then he wasn't. He threatened me. He told me that I'm going to die."

"Hey, calm down," Bryce ordered, "You probably imagined it. I'll go check it out anyway. If there's someone here, I'll find him. You sure you can't describe him?"

"I told you, it was too quick."

"You were probably dreaming," Bryce said soothingly. It's been a long week; we've had a lot going on. Just wait here. I'll go search the house. I'm sure it was nothing."

Leaving his wife to wait with the baby, Bryce began moving quietly from room to room, searching everywhere that a man could possibly hide. He found nothing. The doors and windows were all still as he'd left them, locked and secure. Nobody had broken in.

"Nothing," he yawned returning to his bed, "It was just a dream. Get some sleep, we both need it."

Although the rest of the night was uneventful, Rosetta could no longer sleep. She tossed and turned; her mind unable to shut down. At 7 am, tired and grumpy she rose from her bed to the sound of Tyler's waking cries. Taking him from his cot and slipping downstairs, she quietly prepared a bottle, allowing Bryce another half hour in bed. When he finally came down to join her breakfast was waiting for him on the table.

"I love you; you do know that right?" he said tucking into a cold cereal followed by a couple of warm bagels.

"How are you feeling now about your dream?" he asked once he'd finished eating.

"In the cold light of day, I guess I feel a little stupid," Rosetta replied. "I'm sorry I woke you babe; it was wrong of me."

"Hey, it was nothing. You're ok, that's all that matters," Bryce said. He looked up at the clock on the wall. "I've got to go," he said, wiping his mouth with a napkin. "You be good whilst I'm gone. Try not to get yourself into any mischief." Kissing her goodbye, he grabbed his coat and left the house.

At eleven, Rosetta prepared Tyler another

feed. As he began sucking at the bottle's teat, she recoiled in horror. The milk inside the bottle had turned red. It no longer looked like milk but blood. Snatching the bottle from her baby's mouth, she threw it into the sink and stepped back. Behind her, she thought she could hear a man's voice whispering something to her child. Turning her head, she saw the same shadowy figure from the night before standing next to her baby's highchair.

"Get away from him," she screamed. "Leave him alone." The apparition vanished, dissolving into the air like dust.

Holding her baby in her arms, shaking badly, Rosetta searched the kitchen with her eyes, wondering where the apparition had gone. As she looked over at one corner of the room, she heard laughter. The laughing was deep and cruel. "Who are you?" she yelled asked. "What do you want from me?" The laughter stopped as quickly as it had started.

Rosetta felt dizzy. She knew that she needed to get out of the house. As she picked Tyler from his chair, he began to wail. The poor child was hungry, he still needed feeding. "I'm sorry baby, I'm sorry," she whispered, rocking him gently in her arms. "I'll make you another bottle." She stared over at the sink. The bottle was still there where she'd thrown it. It was filled with milk. There was no blood, there never had been. It was all in her imagination.

"I'm going to take you to nana's," she said rattled by what was happening to her. She was beginning to believe that she might be going mad. Staring down at her baby, blinking away the tears that were beginning to form in her eyes, she forced herself to be strong. "I think you and I need some fresh air," she said pulling Tyler from the chair. "Would you like that? Of course, you would. Mummy has to try to figure out some stuff. It'll only be for a while then we'll come back and have lunch with your Pa ok."

Grabbing her car keys and a few items that her son would need, she headed out to her car. A few feet from her house one of her neighbours was watching her. "Mr. Zuckerman, isn't it?" Rosetta asked, stopping beside her vehicle, and gazing over at him.

"That's right lady."

"Have you lived around here long Mr. Zuckerman?"

"Fifteen years give or take," the old man replied. "Why do you ask?"

"I have to take my son to my mother's house. When I return, I'd like to pick your brain. I've got a few questions I'd like to ask."

"I'm retired. I ain't going nowhere. You come and give me a knock whenever you are ready Mrs. I figure it'll be about the house. Am I right?"

"Yes," Rosetta muttered. "I'll be back soon."

"Of that I'm sure," Zuckerman said watching her strap her baby into the back seat and fixing her with a strange look.

As Rosetta pulled away. Zuckerman's wife joined him by the front gate. "What was that about?" she asked.

"It's starting again," Mr. Zuckerman replied.

~

"As much as I love little Tyler, you have got to understand that I am not your unpaid babysitting service," Rosetta's mother said taking the baby from her daughter's arms. "I think we have done more than enough for you lately, don't you? Perhaps you should think about paying a babysitter or standing on your own two feet for a change?"

"Yes mother," Rosetta apologised. "And I

will, I promise. It's a few hours that's all." She turned and headed toward the door. "You know it's important, otherwise I wouldn't ask."

"Fine," Rosetta's mother said reluctantly.

Half an hour later Rosetta was back outside the Zuckerman's property. As she stretched out her hand to knock on the door, Mr. Zuckerman was already opening it. " "Come on though," he said beckoning her inside.

"You sit dear, and I'll go grab us all a home-made lemonade," Zuckerman's wife said making her way out to the kitchen. She was a big woman with thick grey hair and a kind-looking face. Her husband looked more like a hunter. He was dressed in loose-fitting jeans and a chequered shirt. His face was long and weathered by years out in the sun.

"Sit down, I don't bite," he said. His voice was deep and husky. It sounded like he was growling when he talked.

Rosetta sank onto the single leather seat facing the matching couch upon which Mr. Zuckerman was perched. She waited patiently for his wife to return, restless in the awkward silence. When the old lady returned, she was carrying a tray with three drinks and a plate of cookies.

Placing them on the table, Mrs. Zuckerman sat down beside her husband. Sitting quietly at his side, she waited for the conversation to begin.

"What do you know about my house?" Rosetta asked. "There's something wrong with it isn't there?"

Why do you ask? Has something happened?"

"Yes," Rosetta responded. "There have been one or two things."

"Like what?"

"Oh, it was just simple things at first," Rosetta said feeling n little foolish. "Lights being on when I'd thought I'd turned them off. Objects moved to the wrong place, that sort of thing. But last night..." her voice trailed off.

"Last night you saw something you couldn't explain," Mr. Zuckerman said finishing her sentence for her."

Rosetta nodded. "What's wrong with my house? What do you know about it? Why was it empty for seven years? Why did nobody want to buy it before me?"

"You don't know do you?" Mrs. Zuckerman replied.

"No, I don't, but after last night I've realised

that something's not right about the place."

Mr. Zuckerman cleared his throat. "You ever heard of an artist called Casey John Pickerman?" He asked.

Rosetta shook her head.

"Yeah, I figured as much," Mr. Zuckerman said rubbing his chin. "Well, Mr. Pickerman was the original owner of that house that you now own. He was an artist, not well known, but good by all accounts. For some reason unknown to me, people around here didn't like him. They considered him odd. People would talk about him when his back was turned. They'd whispered things. They seemed to have it in their heads that his artwork was somehow evil, that what he painted was not of this world. Folks said that things seemed to happen to people that bought his works. They died or disappeared with no explanation. A detective of that time believed it so badly, that he started a personal vendetta against Pickerman. Nothing ever stuck though. Detective George Dowdy couldn't prove anything, and it rankled him. He had nothing and he knew it. I mean paintings don't kill people do they, how can they?"

"Dowdy wouldn't let it go of course. He'd

made up his mind. He'd became obsessed. He was determined to prove that Pickerman was evil even if it ended up costing him his career. One day in a fit of rage, he shot and killed Pickerman. A little girl had disappeared a couple of weeks earlier you see. Just days before she vanished, her father had bought one of Pickerman's works. Dowdy decided that the two things had to be connected."

"Wow, that's some story. I'm shocked I've never heard it before. What's your take on it? Was there something in it do you think?"

"Well missy, seems you've already felt his presence in the house, or you wouldn't be talking to me. I guess the real question is what you believe?"

"I don't know, it's a little insane. How can it be true? You know what I think?"

"No, what do you think dear?" Mrs. Zuckerman asked.

"I think I had a bad dream and I'm crazy listening to this. I didn't sleep well, and I've let it get to me. I've moved to a new house, and I'm worn out. I'm letting things get on top of me. Much as I like a good horror story, that's all this is."

"Is it?" Mr. Zuckerman replied. "I can't

make you believe, but I would suggest you think hard about what you saw last night."

"How do you know I saw anything?"

"I don't, but that house is bad. It has a bad history. You have to leave that place."

"You should listen to him, dear. Things happen in that house. It's cursed."

"When did Pickerman die?" Rosetta asked.

"Dowdy killed Pickerman in nineteen sixty-three. He was just twenty-six at the time. The house was empty for a spell after that. I think the first people after Pickerman were the Rosenburg's. Mrs. Rosenburg hung herself three months after moving in. I'm told that Mr. Rosenburg went mad shortly after. That was around nineteen sixty-nine. The house remained empty for another year after that. When the fuss had died down, Mr. William Burrows bought the place. He stayed there for three days then never went back. People say that he saw something in that house that scared him to death."

"Ok, I'm guessing that you are going to tell me that everyone who has bought that house has either died or left... am I right?"

"Look you can fight me all you want, but I'm trying to help you," Mr. Zuckerman said, a grave look on his face. "I can't do that if you won't help yourself. Please take my warning seriously. You are in danger if you stay there. You have to leave."

"What did you say that detective's name was?" Rosetta asked. Something was clicking in the back of her head. "Dowdy, wasn't it?"

"That's right. You know the name?"

"I don't know. It seems familiar like I've heard it before. It's probably nothing." She drank her lemonade and took a cookie. "I think I've taken enough of your time," she said rising from her seat. "Thank you for your hospitality."

"I'd like to show you something before you leave if that's ok," Mrs. Zuckerman said stopping Rosetta as she headed toward the door. She left the room and returned with a black folder. "Take a look," she said handing it to her guest. "It's interesting I can assure you."

Rosetta was intrigued. She returned to her seat and began looking through the pages.

"These are all of the pictures that were taken from that house and archived after Pickerman's death," Zuckerman said, watching Rosetta as she turned the pages. "I found them in the library. Things have to be made public after a certain period. It's some new law they created, freedom of information or something like that. I was always interested in the case, so I took it upon myself to make copies of what I found..."

Rosetta stared at the pictures. They were dark. Most were images of death. A man hanging by the neck from a tree, a graveyard with a hand rising from the earth. There was one particularly nasty picture of a lady screaming with her eyes hanging on her cheeks. The pictures were gruesome and evil.

Mr. Zuckerman watched as Rosetta turned each page, waiting for her to reach the last. When she did, her face had turned completely white.

"That's Tyler," she said trying to get the words out. "But how? Pickerman painted my baby before he was even born. How's that possible. Tyler's even wearing the same romper suit he has on today..." The words stuck in her mouth. Oh my God," she cried out. "My baby is in danger. I have to leave; I have to leave right now."

Mr. Zuckerman grabbed Rosetta's arm as she ran out onto the path outside. "Don't go back to that house." He pleaded. "Promise me you'll never return to that place."

***

When Rosetta arrived at her Grace, her mother's house, she was still shaking. "How is he, how's he been," she said bursting through the door.

"Tyler's fine," Grace cooed. "Go make yourself a drink and rest your feet. Everything's under control here."

Rosetta poured herself an orange juice. Watching her mother playing with the baby out of the corner of her eye, she took out her phone and began searching the internet. She soon found what she was looking for, an old document from the sixties about Pickerman. The document had been written shortly after his death and gave a brief background to his history as well as an account of the mysterious deaths he'd been allegedly liked to. Pickerman had been born in nineteen thirty-seven, the article read. He'd been twenty-six when he died at the hands of Dowdy. The photo of him at the top of the page was in black and white. Rosetta stared at it, trying to make sense of what she was seeing. It was definitely the man she'd seen in her house, but how was it possible?

She held her phone closer, no longer

scared, but instead completely overcome by a deep-seated need to get to the truth. The guy was rather ordinary looking in the cold light of day she thought, studying the photo. His face was bony and long ending above his brow in a Short brown quiff, the popular haircut of the day. He stared out at Rosetta from his picture with deep sad eyes that looked as if they'd lived a troubled life. There was certainly nothing sinister about his appearance, nothing to be frightened of, even so, this was the man that had threatened her the night before. It was also the same man she'd seen in her kitchen, the artist who had miraculously painted her son decades before he'd been born. As Pickerman continued to stare up at her from the screen of her phone, a cold shiver ran the length of her spine.

Rosetta scrolled on to another article. The new reports were about her house. Since Pickerman's death in sixty-three, there had been only eight further owners. All had died or left under mysterious circumstances. In the years that followed, the locals had decided that the house was cursed. Nobody would touch it. Now and then, somebody would look at it, but the house stayed empty.

Who was this man?" Rosetta wondered. Could he be capable of the things that Zuckerman said? it seemed impossible. How could somebody's pictures cause a person to die? She tried to dismiss it from her mind but couldn't. The images from her kitchen rolled over and over in her head. Too much had happened, too many things that she couldn't explain. As much as she would have liked, the bizarre events happening around her property could not easily be ignored.

Rosetta moved her hand ready to close the page then stopped. She had suddenly noticed Pickerman's date of birth. It jumped out at her from the screen like a giant warning beacon. It was April the seventeenth, the same date of birth as her son Tyler's.

"Ma," she said closing the screen and looking over at her mother. "Have you ever heard the name George Dowdy before?"

"Of course, I have honey. He was a detective back in the sixties," her mother replied. "He was the officer who shot dead that mad painter..." She paused for a moment, the concentration leaving deep lines on her brow. "I do believe he's related to us somehow," she said thinking aloud. "I think he was a cousin or something on your father's side."

Rosetta felt faint.

"Are you ok," Rosetta's mother asked noticing her pallor.

"What time is it?" Rosetta asked, trying to swallow the dread she was feeling inside.

"It's nearly one."

"I have to go, Rosetta, said grabbing her keys and heading toward the door. "Bryce will be home anytime now for his dinner break. I'm going to leave Tyler with you if that's ok?"

"Oh no you don't," Mrs. Fielding said waving a finger in the air. "You're not leaving your baby here with me again. I do have a life of my own you know. I have things to do. If you are leaving this house, you are taking your son with you."

"You don't understand, I can't, it's not safe."

"Enough," Rosetta's mother snapped. "Honestly dear, I've heard just about every piece of nonsense that can come out of that mouth of yours. Take your baby home and stop this at once."

Rosetta could see that it was useless arguing. She grabbed baby Tyler and hurriedly made her way to the car.

***

Rosetta drove hard, but the roads were unusually busy. It was as if everybody had jumped into their vehicles at the same time, colluding with one another, conspiring to stop her from getting home. Pushing her way through the streets, negotiating her way through the many obstacles that blocked her way forward, she finally made it to Belmont Street. As she pulled up outside the house, Bryce was already making his way up the path to the house.

"Stop," Rosetta cried, flinging open her door and jumping from the vehicle.

Bryce turned around. "Hi honey," he called out. He was grinning from ear to ear as he made his way back down the path and joined her at the car. Reaching into the back, he unbuckled Tyler's seat and lifted him gently out of the vehicle.

"No," Rosetta screamed. "You can't take him in there."

"Why not?" Bryce enquired, a confused look in his eyes.

"I can't explain it right now, but you have to trust me. There's something wrong with the house."

"Seriously?" Bryce said shaking his head. "Do we have to do this again? I told you last night, it was just a dream for God's sake. There was nobody in the house then and there's nobody in there now."

Striding briskly to the front door, he turned the key and looked back at her over his shoulder. "You coming Rosetta or am I going in alone?"

Rosetta sprinted up the path. As she got near Bryce opened the door and stepped onto the porch. Realising that she had no choice but to follow, Rosetta took a deep breath and reluctantly entered after him. As she made her way inside, an unseen hand reached out and slammed the door behind her.

"Oh dear," Mrs. Zuckerman said, watching the house from her window across the road. "Why didn't they listen to us?" Holding onto her husband's arm, she crossed herself and prayed.

The air around the Kleiser's house began to rumble. The noise grew steadily louder. With a loud crack the ground opened and the house sank into the earth disappearing into the mud as if it had never existed.

"Such a nice couple," Mr. Zuckerman said

shaking his head in disbelief. "If only they'd headed our advice."

On the grass, a few feet from where the house had stood until just moments before, Mrs. Zuckerman had spotted the baby. It lay on its back on the ground dressed in the same baby suit that it had worn when Bryce Klieser had held it lovingly in his arms.

Mr. Zuckerman had seen him too. Opening his front door, he ran out into the street and carefully scooped the young child from the soil. As he hurried away, he thought that he could hear a man's demonic laughter rising from the earth.

THE ALIEN

The middle-aged man imprisoned inside room 14 at the Nathan Holmes Institute wasn't sure how long he'd been there. It could have been days, weeks, or even months for all he knew. During that time, he'd been visited by a whole host of doctors each of them dressed in fancy white uniforms that stank of the starch. All of them were the same. Each man or woman trying to get inside his head to unlock the cause of his mental instability and get a big tick on their resume.

The orderlies that visited him when the doctors weren't around were brutal. They beat him as he lay on his bed trapped and helpless, laughing at his inability to defend himself. Punching him and jabbing at his flesh with nasty-looking syringes, they left bruises and pockmarks on his skin.

Aside from the beatings that he had to endure; the man named John Smith was routinely forced to swallow a large supply of drugs. When he was sedate enough to travel, the doctors would subject him to a host of experimental treatments in the main observation theatre. The treatments he was told, were for his own good. They were given to him to ensure the safety of the public upon his eventual release. In an age when mental health was at the back of every political figure's mind, it seemed that the Nathan Holmes institute either didn't know or didn't care about the changing world around it.

Listening to the footsteps echoing in the corridor outside his room John mentally prepared himself for another session of treatment. Who would it be today, he wondered. Not Doctor Linda Collins he hoped. She was the nastiest of all the other doctors he'd met. She didn't even try to hide her dislike of him. Her attitude was condescending and rude. She was also rather ugly. She reminded John of a reptile. With her thin red hair, long face, and those big bug eyes, she would probably have looked good on the shelf of any pet shop.

John had also noticed when close enough to examine her, that Collin's skin was particularly dry. Maybe it was all the hours spent under the bright fluorescent lights or maybe she just had a bad skin problem. Either way, she'd benefit from the use of a good moisturiser.

As the footsteps stopped outside his door, John tensed. He listened to the swipe card running down through the electronic bracket and braced himself. As the door opened inwards toward him, he let out a sigh of relief. Standing in the open doorway was Doctor Denise Dixon. Unlike her older counterpart, Dixon was interesting to talk to. She was also very easy on the eyes. Younger than her colleague by at least ten years, not only was she a lot prettier, but she smelt good too.

Unfortunately for her, the easy-going approachable style with which Dixon conducted herself were not the qualities that the institute was looking for. Her steadfast refusal to conform to the Holmes doctrine was beginning to irritate her superiors and she knew it. Her days were numbered. It was only a matter of time before she'd be replaced.

"Good morning John, how are you today?" Dixon asked, stepping further into the room flanked by her two orderlies.

"I'm fine now that I know it's you and not the reptile that will be treating me today," John replied looking up at her from his bed.

"Reptile?" Dixon responded.

"Doctor Collins," John said noting the confusion in her eyes.

"I'm sorry, who?" Dixon enquired "Do I know her? The name doesn't ring a bell."

"It's ok, I must have gotten the name wrong," John said letting it drop. He watched nervously as the nearest orderly approached him, ready to unstrap his wrist so that he could administer the sedative he held in his hand.

The orderly's name was Mike Johnson. He was big and powerful like his brutish companion Taylor Prince who stood a couple of feet away holding a menacing black baton in his hand. Both men liked working out. Both men also enjoyed violence. They were two of the thugs that regularly beat him over the slightest provocation. John had quickly learned not to test them. Having felt the pain of their punishment, he was in no mood to provoke them again."

Johnson bent down and unstrapped the leather restraint on John's left arm. Rolling up his sleeve he felt for a vein then forcefully jabbed the syringe into his arm. Twisting his head, he pulled a face at Dixon and tried not to laugh as she shook her head and tutted.

"I don't understand why he has to be strapped to the bed like that. He's not dangerous is he," Dixon said once the sedative had been administered. "And do you have to be so rough all the time? Is it really necessary?

"My job is to keep you, safe lady," Johnson growled. "This guy is a nut job. He might look meek and mild, but don't underestimate him. He tried to bite me when he first arrived here."

"And you did nothing to provoke him I suppose?"

"If you don't like what I do lady," Johnson spat, "Then go tell my boss. You won't like what he has to say though. I'm just following his orders. If you hate this place so much you should go find a position at one of those lovey snowflake institutes that are springing up all over the place. Maybe you can get one of the damned fruitcakes there to polish your nails for you. Hey, with the right incentive you might even be able to train them to apply your lipstick."

Prince broke into laughter. "You crack me up dude," he said slapping his friend on the back between fits of giggles.

"If you two are done, could you please get my patient off the bed so that we can get out of here?" Dixon scowled.

"You're the boss sweetheart," Johnson said stepping around the bed and unstrapping John's other wrist from the metal bracket that was keeping him pinned.

Prince stepped forward and joined his partner. Between them, the two men lifted John from the sheets. Once he'd been given a moment to stretch his arms to relieve his cramp, they marched him forcefully from the room.

"Where are we going?" John asked as they made their way down a series of white corridors that smelt of bleach or some other powerful disinfectant.

"Shut up dickhead," Taylor Prince replied.

118

"Nobody gave you permission to talk, did they?"

"Ignore him, John," Dr. Dixon muttered sympathetically. "We are taking you down to section three. You are going to have an MRI scan. Once we are finished there, you will be taken to see Professor Adam Hall who will be overseeing your treatment today."

"I've already had scans. They found nothing. You are wasting your time," John sighed. "Who's this Hall guy anyway? What does he want to do to now that hasn't been tried already?"

"Last warning nut job..." Prince snarled ignoring Dixon's authority and jabbing his baton into John's side.

"Stop that immediately," Dixon said glaring at the orderly. "Whether you like it or not Mr. Prince, Smith is allowed to speak. I think it would be wise to remember that I am in charge here not you."

"Yeah, but for how long?" Johnson said jumping in to help his friend.

The group continued in silence. A few minutes later they reached some fire doors. Pushing their way through the heavy doors, the small group made their way into section three, an annex built onto the main building. Stopping outside a door, marked MRI scanning room, Johnson pressed the buzzer and stepped back.

Five minutes passed, then another ten. The group huddled uncomfortably together waiting in silence. Finally, the green light went on above the door. A man in a white uniform clicked the buzzer and let them through.

"Is the patient wearing anything metal? Any jewellery, watches, hearing aids, etc" the man asked. He was slim, probably in his early fifties with brown hair that had greyed in one or two places.

"What do you think?" Johnson replied. He glanced over at his partner. "Perhaps we should remove the Rolex we stuffed up his arse earlier eh buddy? Wouldn't want it to ruin the doctor's expensive toy now, would we?"

Prince broke into fits of laughter again.

"Ok," the male nurse said trying to shut out the two men's laughter. "Please put this on." He handed John a hospital robe and stepped back.

John stepped out of his bland two-piece uniform and slipped into the robe with Prince and Johnson watching him like hawk the whole time. Once he was done, he was led over to the huge MRI machine and told to lie down.

120

"There will be a humming sound when you enter that many people find rather unsettling," The nurse said. "You might also feel a little claustrophobic. Please try to ignore it and lay completely still. It will all be over fairly quickly."

John nodded and waited for the process to begin.

"All yours," the nurse said looking up at the viewing room above where a doctor was preparing to start the machine and check the results.

John crossed his fingers and closed his eyes. Lying completely still, he counted down the moments until the machine stopped, forcing himself to shut out the humming sound around him.

The procedure took about twenty minutes, a lot longer than he would have liked. With his nerves in tatters, the session finally came to an end. Once John had re-dressed and the images that had been taken from the scan had been handed to Dr. Dixon, the group got ready to move.

"Ok, let's get out of here," Denise said heading toward the door.

After a trek through even more white corridors, the group arrived at treatment room six somewhere in the main building. Stopping outside the door, Dr. Dixon lifted her hand and knocked gently on the wood.

"Enter, a male voice called out. The voice was deep with a posh upper-class accent. John guessed that the speaker was quite old, maybe in his late sixties or even older. As they entered the room his guess was proved to be right.

Professor Hall was sitting at a large oak table facing the group as they made their way through the open door. His face was gaunt and covered in wrinkles, the result probably of too many days in the sun as a younger man when the dangers of U.V rays had not properly been explored. His thinning grey hair was brushed over sideways in a futile attempt to hide the bald areas of his scalp. A large pair of thick round glasses were propped on the bridge of his nose beneath thick bushy eyebrows. Although the professor was sitting down, John could see by his loose-fitting jacket that the man was painfully thin.

"Come forward, come forward, the professor smiled, pushing himself up from his chair and stepping around the table. "let's not be shy."

"The scans you asked for," Dixon said handing him the MRI results as she stepped closer.

"Thank you," Professor Hall replied taking

the envelope from her outstretched hand.

Glancing at the two burly orderlies, he waved his free hand dismissively and indicated toward the door. "You can go now."

"Can't do that I'm afraid professor," Johnson replied. "We have orders to wait with the patient."

I see," Hall responded. "If they are the instructions, you have been given, I suppose I'll have to adhere to them. I think, however, that it might be prudent to do your waiting outside in the corridor. I wish to afford my patient some privacy whilst I treat him. I will not tolerate you hovering over him like a couple of vultures. Has he been sedated? I presume he has."

Johnson nodded.

"I can assume, therefore, that Smith represents no threat. My colleague and I are on the other side of the door should the worst happen. Is that enough to please your bosses do you think? I'd say that it's a happy compromise."

Johnson looked pissed but he had nothing to come back with. "Come on," he said addressing his partner. "Let's go wait outside." Turning on his heels he silently shuffled from the room with his Prince falling in behind him.

"Alone at last," Hall said removing the scans from the envelope and breathing a sigh of relief. Holding the images toward the light, he studied them for a moment then passed them over to Dixon.

"Your thoughts?" he asked.

"I'm not sure," Dixon replied examining the scans closely.

In the cerebellum, the region of the brain responsible for coordinating movement and balance, the young doctor could just make out a tiny circular black shadow. The shadow was so small it was almost unnoticeable. Even so, both she and the professor had spotted it.

"Could it be a glitch in the machine?" she asked looking up and meeting Hall's eyes.

"I don't know," the professor replied honestly. "The pictures suggest that some sort of foreign body is resting against the brain tissue, but logic tells me otherwise."

He looked over at his patient. "Have you been involved in an accident Mr. Smith, either recently or sometime in your past? Has anything happened to you that could have resulted in some kind of head trauma?"

"Not that I'm aware of," Smith replied.

"And unfortunately, we have no medical records to refute that," Hall sighed.

Smith shrugged. "Sorry about that."

Hall moved away from his table and made his way over to his patient. Taking Smith's head gently in his hands he carried out a quick examination of the back of his head and neck then returned to his seat.

"I think I'm inclined to agree with your observation doctor," he said settling back into the chair. "It is much more likely to be a glitch in the machine than anything else. A major injury of the type that resulted in a foreign object embedding itself in Smith's cerebellum seems very implausible. Such an injury would almost certainly have killed him. There are no signs of scarring on his head or neck, nothing to indicate that such an accident has occurred. I think, therefore, that we can safely rule it out. I will examine the scans in more depth later when I am alone, of course just to be sure that I've missed nothing. I will also contact maintenance and get them to check that the machine is working properly. If no faults are found, I'll set up a slot for another scan so that we can put this thing to bed."

"Now then," he said addressing John Smith,

"I think we should get better acquainted, don't you? I've been itching to meet you ever since you arrived here."

"And when was that exactly?" Smith asked taking a seat opposite the professor and making himself comfortable. "I have no idea."

"Of course," Hall apologised. You have no clock in your room. How remiss of me. You must have absolutely no concept of time. If it helps, you've been here for nearly a month," he mumbled.

I figured it must be something like that," John said rubbing at the stubble on his chin, "but it feels so much longer.

"I suppose it would, and I can see that you are upset. I imagine that I'd probably be the same were the shoe on the other foot. But I am here now, and I want to help. If you'll agree to co-operate, I'll do my best to get you released. How does that sound?"

"It sounds nice professor. But please don't make promises that you can't keep."

"I'll try my best," Hall replied. He paused for a moment as if deep in thought. "You look nothing like I imaged," he said. "Your appearance is very ordinary; one might even say mundane would you not agree?

"What were you expecting professor? Did you think I'd have a long-elongated face, big eyes, and pointy ears?"

"Of course not," Hall laughed. "I'm actually very pleased by what I see. Your baldness, that rather endearing chubby little face...it adds a certain depth to your somewhat fascinating story. The fact that there is nothing alien about your appearance almost makes it that more believable wouldn't you agree."

"Hey, watch it, professor," Smith growled. "Your remarks are quite offensive. I do have feelings you know."

"I'm sorry," Hall apologised. "I didn't mean to insult you. I was just trying to make a point."

"And you made it."

"What is it that you want from me, professor?" he asked after an uneasy silence. "Are you here to help me, or are you just hoping to make a name for yourself?"

"I want to help you, dear boy. I'm a bit too old in the tooth for playing games," Hall replied.

"Then can we just get on with whatever it is that you are intending to do?"

"Yes of course."

Picking up a black binder from his desk, the professor thumbed it open, then ran his fingers delicately down one of the pages. "Your notes state that you were arrested on the eleventh of April and that you were apprehended inside the home of Mr. and Mrs. Thwaits, number twenty-four Tenby Hill Coventry. Is that correct?" he asked.

"Apparently."

"It says here that you cut a lock of hair from the heads of the Thwaites two sleeping children. You then took a couple of toothbrushes from the bathroom before heading into the main bedroom to steal a hairbrush."

"I've been over this..."

"Mr. Thwaites awoke to the sound of your footsteps by his bed and overpowered you..."

"Yes, yes, and yes."

"Mr. Thwaites wife called the police," Hall continued "You were then taken to Coventry police station and searched. Aside from the children's hair that I mentioned earlier, you had upon your person a small number of polythene bags. One of these bags contained a green mug. Another had a couple of carefully wrapped wine glasses. Eight smaller bags had more human hair inside, plus the toothbrushes and several cigarette butts."

"Why are we doing this? You already know the information inside that folder. I'm sure you've read it several times am I correct?" Smith complained.

"Yes, I have," the professor replied, "But I'm simply attempting to make sure that I have my facts right."

Smith scowled at him.

"May I continue?" Hall asked as his patient eyeballed the floor, refusing to look up at him.

"Do what you want," Smith mumbled.

"Why did you inform the arresting officer that the items he confiscated were to be used to conduct a series of tests?"

"You tell me?"

"Officer Boyd writes in his report that you imply that you've been sent to Earth by your superiors with specific orders to collect human DNA. Your task apparently, is to assess whether it is a compatible match to your species. Concerned by your statement, he handed you over to a psych councillor to assess your mental state. Have I missed anything at all?" Hall asked quietly.

"No, I think you covered it."

"And you still insist that you remember none of this?"

John nodded.

"I think you are lying to me," Hall said accusingly. "I think you still believe that you are an alien. I also believe that you are faking your amnesia. You think that if you can keep up your charade, we'll simply write you off and release you. Is that not the truth Mr. Smith?"

"No," Smith replied angrily. "I'm sick of this shit. How many times am I going to be asked these same bloody questions? Do I have to keep repeating myself?"

"I understand your anger John, but I can't help you if you won't help yourself. Pretending that you don't remember anything isn't going to help you get out of here any faster. I promised you that I would take a different approach to your treatment, and I stand by that. If I'm to proceed further, I need to know as much information about you as possible."

John clenched his teeth in frustration. "I'm sorry professor. I can't help you. He responded."

"You're not going to get anything out of him professor. I'm afraid you are wasting your time with these questions," Dixon interjected. "John has kept to the same script every time he's been questioned. He always says the same thing, never deviates. It's as if he has realised the trouble that he is in and shut down to save himself. We've been trying to break him for almost a month and failed to make any progress at all."

The professor nodded. "Well, we'll just have to take a different approach then won't we."

"Feel free professor," John replied sarcastically, "Do what you have to do, but it honestly won't help."

"Your name John smith... is it real or is it made up?" Hall asked. "I presume it is the latter."

"I don't know professor. You tell me. You seem to be the one with all the bloody answers."

"I am not your enemy," Hall said annoyed by John's refusal to help himself. "Putting up barriers and playing games will not help you. Why are you lying to me? Are you afraid, is that it? Has somebody hurt you since you've been here?"

John thought about Linda Collins again. He closed his eyes and visualised the first time she'd entered his room. She'd been alone at the time which had surprised him. He still clearly remembered the threats she'd whispered into his ear. As he'd lain on his bed helpless and vulnerable, she'd smiled at him. The smile had sent shivers down his spine. Unable to run, he watched helplessly as she'd stuck a large needle into his neck knowing that there was nothing, he could do to protect himself. The woman was evil, plain, and simple.

Snapping his eyes open, John looked back up at the professor. "Nobody," he lied.

"I'm sorry, I simply don't believe you," Hall sighed. "I think somebody has frightened you. I know the reputation of this place. I am quite aware of what goes on here. My guess would be those two brutes standing outside the door have something to do with your reluctance to talk to me. I could have them removed if it would make you feel more comfortable."

"Do I look like a victim?" John growled! "I assure you that I am not. Nor am I a liar. Maybe I did say those things you accuse me of, but If I did, I wasn't in control at the time."

"So, you admit it now?"

"I admit nothing. Stop putting words into my mouth."

"I'm sorry," Hall apologised. "Look, this is

all getting a little heated. Let's take five and start again, shall we?"

"Without the insults?"

"Yes, without the insults," the professor promised.

Hall left the room. After a quick recess, he returned ready to restart the conversation. "Ok John crunch time," he said resuming his previous position against the table, "Like it or not, the management team here has gone out of the way to help you. They are running out of patience. Despite the many background checks that have been conducted and the blood and saliva samples that have been taken, we are no nearer to finding out who you are or where you came from. Your fingerprints, your dental records, they all lead to nothing. You do not appear to exist. We simply cannot find you on any known database. It makes no sense. What are you hiding? How have you managed to stay off the radar for so long? It's practically impossible not to show up somewhere in this day and age, yet somehow you have managed to achieve what others cannot. You appear to have no history. You are a ghost. How have you done it?"

"you tell me, professor? Where did I come

from?" Smith asked. He was smiling with a mischievous gleam in his eyes.

"I don't know," Hall replied. "There is something very strange going on here. I have no doubts about that. Your story in any other circumstances would be laughable. Your total lack of history makes me wonder though. I just can't shake the feeling that there is more going on here than meets the eye. I believe that you are a far more complex individual than you are letting on."

"Guess you'll never know," Smith teased.

"My God," Dixon whistled, listening to the exchange between the two men. "You actually believe he's an alien, don't you?"

"At this point, I'm not sure what I believe," Hall responded, "But I think it is healthy to keep an open mind. I have lived long enough to know that sometimes the truth can be far stranger than fiction. Things aren't always black or white."

Dixon burst into laughter. Wiping away a tear with the back of the hand she turned to her patient. "I'm so sorry," she apologised. "If I'd known what was going through the professor's mind, I wouldn't have brought you down here. I'll call m superiors at once and request that this session be brought to an end."

"That's not necessary," Smith said shaking his head, "I'm rather curious to hear what the professor is going to do next. I'd like to stick around if you don't mind."

"Yes of course," Dixon responded, "If that's what you wish."

"So, what do you intend to do with me, professor?" Smith asked.

"Oh, it's quite simple John," Hall replied, loosening his tie and unbuttoning his top shirt button, "I'm going to attempt to hypnotise you. I want to see what lurks inside your mind."

"I don't think that's a good idea," Smith muttered. The smile had suddenly gone from his face, he looked worried.

"I'm inclined to agree with my patient," Dixon said watching John shifting uncomfortably in his chair. "Recent studies have shown that hypnotism doesn't produce the positive results that we used to believe, that instead it merely plants ideas into the subject's head, causing him or her to react to the stimuli being fed to them.

"I have read the papers you refer to," the professor snapped, "They infuriate me. The men that wrote them are narrow-minded idiots. I have been practising this type of therapy for over thirty-five years. I have had nothing but good results. I think my record speaks for itself."

"What do you want me to do?" Dixon asked turning to Smith. "Do you want me to end this?"

"No. Let him play," John responded. "If he wants this so bad, let him have it. Just remember though, whatever happens, it's not on me."

Hall ignored the warning. Brushing it aside, he turned his head and indicated towards a leather chair on the other side of the room. "Please go and make yourself comfortable," he instructed.

John Smith got up and walked over to the leather seat.

"I need you to relax and clear your mind," Hall said removing a small rectangular-shaped object from a shelf on the wall. Approaching the chair, he held it out in front of him allowing John Smith to see it.

John gazed at the pendulum then at the professor, curious as to whether such a thing could put him to sleep. Relaxing into his seat he attempted to clear his head of all the thoughts bouncing around, but it was useless. The room was too bright. The lights hurt his eyes. "Do you think you could turn them down?" he asked.

"Yes of course," Hall responded.

Making his way over to his desk, he closed the drapes on the window and returned to his patient. Plugging in a standing lamp by John's chair, the professor re-positioned the head, then switched it on. With the smaller light now focused solely on the chair, Denise Dixon turned off the room's main lights.

"Now concentrate on the object you see before you," Hall said holding the pendulum loosely in his hands. "Focus on the pendulum and nothing else."

John did as he was instructed. He watched the arm swing back and forth, listening to its gentle rhythm, controlling his breathing.

"In a moment you will start to feel tired," the professor whispered. You will feel your body become lighter. All of the negative energy will wash away and leave you."

John smith closed his eyes. He did indeed feel tired. He fought against it but failed.

"When I click my fingers you will sleep," the professors' voice drifted in his ears. "In three, two, one... sleep."

Smith's eyes were closed tight. He looked relaxed, his body completely still.

"Who am I speaking to?" Hall asked, watching him closely.

"Kylisztian."

"Is that your real name?"

"Yes and no."

"I'm confused," the professor said not understanding. "What do you mean?"

"I am Kylisztian, but I am also John Smith," Smith replied.

"Explain?"

"Kylisztian is my master's body. I am a replicant shaped in his form. I am a synthetic copy, a body that is both machine and man. I have my host's memories, his emotions. I feel what he feels, but I am separate."

The professor was quiet for a moment. He glanced over at Dixon, who was staring back at him with a shocked look in her eyes.

"You were arrested, John. Do you remember that?"

Smith nodded.

"Do you remember why you were arrested?"

"Yes. I was caught removing objects from the human's house."

"Why did you need those objects? What made you take them?"

138

"I took them so that I might conduct my tests."

"What sort of tests?"

"My orders were to gather samples of human DNA and analyse your gene structure."

"For what purpose?"

"Compatibility."

"Are you implying that your gene structure is close to our own?

Smith nodded.

"What is the true purpose behind your mission? Why do you need to know if our two species are compatible?" Hall asked, trying to mask the excitement in his voice.

"My master's race is dying; the women are struggling to produce eggs. The population is dangerously thin. Our planet teeters on the brink of an extinction event. Your race could be the key to our survival."

"Does your master intend to make contact if our genes prove compatible?"

"I do not have that information," Smith replied.

"It's a simple yes or no."

"I do not have that information," Smith repeated.

"Good God man, you must know something," Hall growled. Are there more of you out there?"

"I don't..."

"Yes, you don't have that information," Hall said cutting him off mid-sentence. "I think I'm beginning to understand.

"Ok, so we've learned that your race has fertility problems. You've tested our DNA and you believe that our people are the key to your salvation. What happens next? You can't just land here and expect us to comply with any demand you make upon us. Don't you think that our women would have something to say about that? And what about the germs we carry in our bodies? Are you not concerned about the diseases that we might carry?"

"Yes of course," Smith replied. "That is why I was also tasked with analysing the ecological and biological systems of your world. My people are keen to learn what bugs lie in your systems and what antibodies you possess. If your Earth proves compatible with our own, our scientists will begin to manufacture cures and antibodies to protect our people. "

"Who the hell do you think you are?" Dixon yelled from across the room. Her face was flushed. Her eyes blazed with a mixture of shock and fury. She'd not believed Smith's story in the beginning, but as Hall's session rolled on, she was quickly coming to realise that the professor had been right all along. The hairs rose on the back of her neck as the cold ugly truth began to dawn on her.

Hall waved his hand and glared in her direction, worried that her outburst had put his session in jeopardy. Looking down at John Smith, he was relieved to notice that his eyes were still closed. Checking to make sure that his breathing was steady and not erratic, he lowered his voice and re-started his questioning.

"Where is your home, John?" he said softly. "Where do you come from?"

"Many lights years from here. You will not see it amongst the stars in your sky."

"How did you get here?"

"I was dropped onto your surface by a Patheon aerial vehicle, serial number D44378."

"And where did this vehicle come from? Where is it now?"

"The Patheon is a two-seat aerial shuttle. It came from the mother ship. The vehicle returned once its cargo was released."

"How do you intend to make contact with your ship once you have completed your mission? You have no radio, no communication devices. Are you telepathic perhaps?"

"No."

"Then how?"

"I am not permitted to say."

"You can tell me, John. Are we not friends after all?"

"You are not my friend. It is forbidden."

"Ok John," Hall said scratching his head, "Let's try something else, shall we? You told me earlier that you are a replicant, that your host is Kylisztian. You said that you have his memories. Were you telling the truth?"

"Yes."

"I'd rather like to explore some of those memories if you'd be willing. I think it would help you. Would that be acceptable?"

Smith nodded.

"That's good. Look over to your left. There is a long dark corridor beside you. Do you see it?"

"John's eyes moved beneath their lids. "Yes," he replied.

"In the distance, there is a light," Hall whispered, "I want you to walk toward it. The light is taking you back. It is taking you further and further...""Ok, Stop. Who am I talking to?" He said after a brief pause.

"My name is Kylisztian."

"Hello, Kylisztian. It's nice to meet you. My name is Adam Hall. Can you tell me where you are?"

"I'm in a white room."

"Where is this room?"

"It's in the dome."

"What is the dome Kylisztian? Why are you there."

"You can call me Kylis if you like sir. All my friends do."

"Ok Kylis. I'll do that. Tell me about the dome? What is it? Is it close to your home?"

"No. My home is in the Bazan. It is close to the purple mountains. The dome is in the Palioz Zone north of the first city.

"How old are you Kylis?"

"I am eight moons."

"I see. And why are you not at school?"

"What is a school?" Smith asked.

"Somewhere you go to learn."

"Oh," Smith laughed. "You mean a streaming house. You use strange words."

"I suppose I do. Kylis, tell me about the dome. Is it an extension of a streaming house?

Smith shook his head. "The dome is the place they take you to be upgraded. Mother has taken me because she wants me to be better."

"Is she not happy with how you are doing in the streaming house? Are you falling behind?"

"My instructors say I am bright, but my mother is worried."

"Why?"

"Father is a star pilot. He wants me to join him. He wants me to be like him when I'm older. Mother doesn't want the same thing. She says too many people get hurt. She wants me to take a different path. She wants me to work in science. She says that our planet needs great minds to survive."

"What you want Kylis?"

"I just want to make everyone happy," Smith replied.

Professor Hall was watching John's face. His eyes were moving back and forth beneath his eyelids. His expression was one of deep anguish.

"Are you ok?" Hall asked. "Is something

wrong?"

John Smith wrinkled his nose. His mouth moved from side to side, but he didn't answer. He appeared to be fighting an internal battle with himself.

"Kylis? Are you still there?"

"Yes."

"What is happening?"

"The men with the masks are here," Smith whispered. "I think they are getting ready to put me to sleep. The big man with the green eyes says that when I wake up, I'll be fixed."

"Do you want to be fixed?"

"I don't know. I'm frightened. I just want to go home."

"It's ok, you don't need to be afraid, I won't let them hurt you."

"Promise?

"I promise. Tell me about your upgrade Kylis. What do you know about it?"

"Mother says it will help me because I am slow. She says that the upgrade will make my brain work faster. Father says that she is wrong about me. I hear them arguing. They think I can't hear them, but I can. I know that they can't afford the treatment anyway as they don't have enough credits. Mother doesn't care. She says that they'll find the extra credits somewhere. She says that I must have the upgrade if I'm to reach my full potential. I don't know what that word potential means Mr, but I know it is important. Do you know what it means? I don't want them to fight anymore."

"It just means that your mother wants you to be the best you can be," Hall responded.

Smith's eyes were moving frantically. "I have to go, sir," he said. His voice trembled as he spoke. "They are ready for me now. They are going to put me to sleep. I shouldn't keep them waiting. I don't want to make them angry."

"I understand," Hall replied. He looked down at his patient, his eyes wide with excitement. He was beginning to realise that Smith was unlike anything he'd ever come across before. Even Dixon standing over by the table a few feet away had sensed it.

"Ok, listen to me Kylis," the professor mouthed. "I am going to take you out of that room. The men who wanted to put you to sleep are gone. You don't need to be frightened anymore. Beside you is that long corridor we spoke of. I want you to step back into it and follow the light just like you did before."

Smith nodded.

"You are passing forward in time. You are now an adult. The date is April the eleventh. The year is two-twenty-one. Do you understand the significance of that date Kylis?"

"Yes. It is six days before your people imprisoned me."

"Where are you Kylis. What do you see around you?"

"I am in room six. I am on the upper deck, quadrant four. I am being prepared."

"Prepared for what?"

Smiths' eyes snapped open. "Yes, I understand," he said, his voice suddenly louder, more aggressive than before. "Initiating Defence sequence, time to detonation two minutes. Please enter primary code to deactivate."

Hall looked over at Dixon. "Who's he speaking to?" he mouthed; the shock was written all over his face. Dixon stared back at him. She shook her head and shrugged her shoulders unsure of what to do.

"Kylis, who are you talking to?" Hall asked, an anxious look in his eyes.

"I am not Kylis. I am system nine," Smith responded. "Detonation in one minute forty-three seconds."

"Ok John, I don't know what is happening here, but I am going to bring you out of your trance now. When I count to three you will wake. One two three..."

"One minute and thirty-two seconds until detonation," Smith said ignoring the instruction and continuing the countdown.

"What the hell?" the professor muttered. "Do you think he has a bomb? Could we have missed it? I think need to call bomb disposal and evacuate the building."

"It's impossible," Dixon stammered. "He's playing with you. He's probably been awake the whole time. Where could he possibly hide a weapon? He's been under close supervision since he got here. He has nothing but the clothes we provided him with."

"The scan," Hall said thinking aloud. "There was a foreign body in his cerebellum. We both saw it. We put it down to a glitch in the machine. Do you remember?"

Dixon nodded. She looked nervous. What if the professor was right? The thought was making her extremely uncomfortable. "If the foreign body is a bomb, it can't be that powerful, can it? Surely it can't cause any real damage?" she muttered, wanting to believe her own words. Her mouth was dry, it felt like her tongue might stick to her mouth.

"I don't know. Can we afford to risk it?" Hall responded.

Dixon shook her head. She was beginning to feel a little feint. "I'll sound the alarm," she said turning and reaching for the door. As she grabbed at the handle there was a loud cracking sound behind her like a tree branch breaking. She looked around in time to see Smith's head explode and something black burst out of the back of his skull. His corpse dropped onto the carpet with the object rolling onto the floor and coming to a stop amongst the blood and brain tissue where Smith's head should have been.

Hall's mouth opened and closed. "That can't be what we saw in the scan can it?" he said staring at the black ball with a mixture of horror and disgust. "it's much bigger than I'd imagined."

"I don't know" Dixon croaked. She'd turned pale and was shaking badly.

"Go find some help," Hall ordered realising that she was in a bad way. "tell Prince and Johnson to evacuate the building. Tell them to alert the police and call bomb disposal."

Dixon did as instructed. Taking the orderlies with her, she ran from the room relieved to be able to get away from the macabre scene behind her. The image of the dead man with his brain scattered across the carpet played over and over in her head refusing to leave her as she sprinted down the corridors yelling at people to get away.

Left alone in the room with only Smith's dead body as company, Hall decided to use the opportunity to study the strange object further. As he crouched low and wiped the blood from his glasses, he noticed that the object had grown. Placing his spectacles back onto the bridge of his nose he leaned in closer, curiosity getting the better of him. He recoiled in shock as the object began to vibrate and whine. As the sound grew louder, so did the ball. Within seconds it had grown to the size of a football. Sensing something bad was about to happen the professor pushed himself up from the floor and attempted to run. He never made it.

The object exploded. It ripped through the building like a small nuclear bomb. The walls were blown apart as if they were made of balsa wood. The shock wave spiralled outward, wreaking havoc across a two-kilometre square path. Cars were flung into the air like toys as the powerful blast tore across the city pummelling buildings and reducing everything to rubble.

When the last shock wave subsided and the dust cloud began to settle, the air was filled with the wailing of sirens and the cries of the wounded. Ambulances raced into the area as police, fire, and army crews attempted to cordon off the surrounding streets. Thousands were dead. Even more, lay maimed and bleeding on the pavements and in the roads. Others trapped inside crushed and battered buildings called for help, their cries unheard in the chaos around them.

****

The lone female figure that stood on the hill was unusually quiet. From her perch overlooking the broken back of the city, she watched the choking black smoke cloud that rose into the morning sky. She didn't smile, nor did she revel in the devastation below. As the acrid fumes of fire and death rolled toward her saddling a gentle spring breeze, she closed her eyes and whispered something into the wind. Before her words had faded away, a bright light shone down from the sky illuminating the trees behind her with its powerful beam. The light moved slowly across the grass coming to rest above her head and bathing her body in its' blinding glare. As she raised her arms and tilted her head back the light disappeared. When it was gone completely, so too had the woman who'd stood beneath. Moments later, above the thin canopy of trees, a silver craft shot up into the sky disappearing through the clouds like a bullet.

***

"System eight, welcome back," the bald man in the silver and red two-piece suit smiled. "I take it you have the information we need?"

"Affirmative," Linda Collins replied.

"Good. Please begin download."

Collins took a lead from the case she was holding in her right hand and plugged it into a vein close to her elbow.

"What happened to system nine?" the man called Kylisztian asked, watching his console, "Why did he activate the emergency protocol?"

"He didn't," Collins replied, "I did."

"Why?"

"Nine's internal computer failed. I had no alternative but to intervene."

"I see. What happened?"

"System nine was apprehended by local enforcement shortly after deposition. Whilst in custody he malfunctioned."

"You couldn't fix the problem?"

"I tried but his sensors failed. It took time to re-locate him."

"He talked to their people?"

Collins nodded.

"How much do they know of our plans?"

"They don't. Although system nine's internal matrix was compromised, the damage was not significant. I managed to re-route some of the memory lines. Nine reverted to cover story two as programmed."

"I see," Kylisztian responded. "Would you like to tell me why you didn't shut him down? If you were aware that there was a problem, would it not have been prudent to have deactivated and reported the problem to station 1."

"I tried. His internal matrix overrode me. I assessed the situation and reacted accordingly."

"You deviated from programme parameters and worked the problem on your own?"

"Affirmative master."

"That good."

"My sensors indicate that you are unhappy," Collins said watching her master's face. "Verbally you have praised me, but your expression says otherwise. Have I done something wrong?"

"Yes and no," her master sighed. "I am happy that you have inherited the ability to think freely and to make your own decisions. It is one of the traits that makes you almost human. Unfortunately, you have not yet learned empathy, nor have you gained the knowledge to differentiate between what is right and what is wrong. I'd rather hoped you would."

Please explain," Collins replied. "If I have acted in error, I wish to learn so that I might eliminate future mistakes."

"The decision to activate the device in nine's head, it was the wrong one." Kylisztian replied.

"But is that not the reason you designed me?" Collins asked.

"Yes, it is," Kylisztian replied. "But that doesn't make it right. What you did this morning, what I programmed you to do, it was a mistake. Our actions resulted in the deaths of thousands of people. There will be consequences. I'd

154

hoped that you would have learned that lesson on your own. I guess I just hoped for too much."

"What's going on here?" Canzalok, a senior officer with dark hair and pale blue eyes asked watching the exchange and strolling over.

"Nothing at all Canzalok," Kylisztian responded. Addressing Collins he said, "Thank you system eight. This discussion is finished. Please report to maintenance and close down. Your battery will need recharging. I'll be along in a while to run a full diagnostic."

"Yes master," Collins replied turning away.

"What was that about really, Canzalok?" asked. I'm not stupid. Are you up to something? You know I'll find out if you are."

"Not at all," Kylisztian replied. "Everything is fine here. All our tests have come back positive. I am very pleased with the results. All of the models appear to be working beautifully."

"And the detonation this morning, was that part of your testing procedure?"

"Yes," Kylisztian lied.

Canzalok didn't seem convinced.

"You took a big risk," the officer said thinking aloud, "And why you made one of those things look like you is beyond me."

"It was just a bit of fun," Kylisztian said, trying to laugh it off. "You know us science types."

"Well, your vanity could easily have compromised our mission. Be more careful in the future. No more games. Is that clear?"

"Yes sir, no more games."

"I'm taking it that Collins' reaction to nine's malfunction was what you'd hoped for?" Canzalok asked. "The wingman protocol you set up worked as you'd planned?"

"It most definitely did," Kylisztian replied. The decision to work them in pairs worked even better than I'd expected."

"Good, then we'll proceed as planned. I'll inform the senate. We'll begin the invasion at once. Your mother would be proud," he said smiling. "If she were still alive, she'd applaud you for what you have achieved here today."

Kylisztian wasn't so sure. If she were watching him, she'd probably be rolling in her grave. All those years studying science and genetics had brought him to this. He was a murderer just like the rest of his kind. He might not be pulling the trigger, but it was his mind that had created the killing machines that would set planet Earth on fire. He felt ashamed. His mother would have wanted peace. She pushed him into science so that he'd be able to make a difference. In the end, he'd taken the same route as his father, he'd let her down.

"Do we have to do this?" he whispered looking into Canzalok's face. "Can we not find another way?"

"It is out of my hands. The decision has been made. Because of your work, we will take this feeble planet. The drought that has plagued our people will be over. We are on the brink of something beautiful here. Rejoice my friend. You will be celebrated. Your gift will bring new light to the darkness that has been our unwelcome companion for too long."

"I think that you are placing too much faith in my toys," Kylisztian argued. "The Earthlings may not be as stupid as you believe them to be. When they realize what we are up to they will fight."

"It's already too late. They've lost and they don't even know it. Hundreds of your replicants are already in position. Even more, are ready to be delivered, each one with the power to bring a city to its knees. What could go wrong? As man turns against man and the world he knows falls to ruin, he'll look to his God for salvation. Instead, he'll find us."

Kylisztian was worried. Had he done enough to slow the tide of madness? The replicant's ability to think for themselves had given him a window of hope but would it be enough? Did they possess the ability to fight their programming? Could they gain the knowledge to differentiate between love and hate? It was a big thing to ask. They were just machines after all.

Canzalok was talking again. "Don't look so glum," he smiled. This is a big day for us all. I'll go get some drinks and then you can help me celebrate."

As he turned away and headed off the deck, Kylisztian shuddered. A war was coming, and many would die before it was over.

"To us, to our people, "Canzalok said returning with the drinks. "To us," Kylisztian mumbled.

DEMON FIRE

Jason Ruiz knew he was in trouble. He'd known it the moment he'd stepped out of the store. The three guys waiting on the sidewalk knew it too. They stood huddled together watching him, enjoying his fear, their beady eyes and their body language giving their intentions away.

Jason had seen their type before. He'd lived in New York long enough to recognize the signs. The guys were gang members and he'd just made himself a target.

Realizing that he couldn't walk back into the

store, that the owner would more likely shoot him for bringing trouble to his door than help, he stepped down onto the curb and began walking. His heart thumped heavily in his chest as he made his way down the street hoping that he'd got it all wrong and that the gang meant him no harm. Quickening his pace, he strained his ears and listened for the sound of footsteps. Sure enough, the gang was following.

"Damn it," Jason muttered under his breath. Why had he agreed to come out at such a late hour? How could he have been so stupid! The streets had always been dangerous at night. He knew that. He should have made his mother wait. Her drinking was getting out of hand anyway. Why should he care if she had to go a night without, the guys behind him wouldn't. All they'd care about was what he had in his wallet. Having spent his last twenty bucks on an illegally purchased bottle of whisky that he should never have been served in the first place, his pockets were empty.

Scared out of his wits, desperate for a way to get out of the mess he'd gotten himself into he ran.

"Hey where do you think you're going fuck

head?" he heard one of the gang shout out behind him, "we want to talk to you."

A cold chill ran the length of Jason's spine. He swung his head around, looking toward the road hoping to spot a passing police cruiser, hoping to get lucky but nobody was coming to his aid, not tonight.

Cars passed by; the driver's oblivious of the game playing out just feet away. If anyone did know what was going on they certainly didn't show it. Nobody stopped, nobody tried to help.

In a sheer state of panic, Jason did something foolish. He decided to duck into an alleyway that ran between an all-night takeaway and a grocery store. It was a bad mistake. The alleyway was a dead end. A high metal fence had been erected blocking any chance of escape.

Realizing that he was trapped, Jason glanced nervously at the trash bins and metal skips lined up against the right-hand wall. Maybe he could hide, maybe the gang wouldn't realize he was there if he kept quiet and still? An inner voice told him that he was being stupid. The bins were all full. Even if he could climb inside one of them, the gang would surely work it out. They'd have seen him run into the alley. They'd know he had no place to go. All they'd have to do is search through the trash.

The only way out was the fence. If he could traverse it before the gang caught up, he might still have a chance. Sprinting toward it, he heard the sound of Running footsteps echoed off the walls around him. The gang had entered the alley. He'd run out of time.

"Give it up dude. You've got nowhere to go," the leading gang member shouted. He was tall and skinny with dark hair and pale skin that was pot marked as if he'd had a bad case of acne at some point in his past. He was holding a gun in his right hand and leering at Jason with a huge grin on his face.

"Hand over your wallet," he said moving closer. "This doesn't have to end badly if you behave yourself. You give us what we want, we'll let you live. We're not bad people."

The guys' companions moved up either side of their leader forming a wall, cutting off Jason's last chance of escape. Like the thug with the gun, they were wearing the black leather jackets of the infamous Serpent street gang.

"Please, I don't have anything to give you," Jason begged. "I just spent my last few bucks in the store. It was all the money I had. I have nothing left…"

"You're lying bitch," the gang leader snarled.

"I'm not, I promise. Here take the whisky, you can have it."

"Is this guy for real?" one of the other gang members asked. He was smaller than his buddy and heavily built. He was wearing a red bandana that covered most of his blonde hair. His neck was covered in tattoos. He stared at Jason with eyes full of hate.

"Please, I'm telling you the truth," Jason whimpered.

"Then I guess this just isn't your lucky day," one of the thugs replied.

"Leave the kid alone…" The voice had come from somewhere behind the gang. Someone else was in the alley.

The three gang members whirled around ready to confront the new enemy. "This ain't your fight dude," the guy nearest the trash said pulling a flick knife from his pocket. Unlike his two buddies, his head was shaved completely bald. His skin was heavily tattooed and full of piercings. "Walk away while you still have a chance," he said springing the blade.

The stranger didn't move. He stood still sizing up his three opponents.

"Are you stupid?" the gang leader said stepping forward. He stared at the stranger and extended his gun hand so that the intruder could see the weapon he was holding clearly in the murky light. "I think my friend just told you to leave. Perhaps you have bad hearing. Do you need him to tell you again?"

"No, I heard what he said," the stranger replied. "But I can't do what you ask. Not unless the kid wants me to." He looked past the gang leader's shoulder toward Jason. "Do you want me to leave?" he asked.

Jason stared at him wild-eyed. What the hell was he playing at? Did the guy have a death wish or something? Was he mad? He certainly didn't look like a fighter. He looked more like a businessman. He was dressed in a grey suit. His hair was slicked back and neatly styled. Even so, there was something in his eyes, something dark. As Jason looked into his face a cold chill ran the length of his spine causing the hackles on his skin to rise.

"Kid do you want me to leave?" The stranger repeated. His voice was calm. It carried no sense of urgency. In the dim light with the threat of violence hanging in the air, the question almost seemed surreal.

"You got some balls Mr, I'll give you that," the gang leader said raising his gun higher and pointing it between the stranger's eyes. "But you made a big mistake coming in here."

"Seems to me that you are the one making the mistake," The stranger responded, "But if you let the kid go you can still get out of this alive."

The three gang members burst into laughter. The laughter was forced. The men's faces twitched as the realization dawned that the stranger wasn't afraid of them. Jason could feel the menace oozing from his body even from where he was standing. If he could feel it the gang had to be feeling it too.

"Kid I can help you, but you have to ask," the stranger repeated.

"Ok," Jason said, grateful to have a friend. "I don't know who you are, but if you can get me out of here, I'll do whatever you ask."

The stranger smiled. "Then it is done. The contact has been agreed. You have made it of your own free will. Now that you are marked the contact cannot be undone."

Jason felt a sharp burning sensation between his thumb and forefinger. He looked down. There was a red mark in the shape of a trident burned into his skin. It looked inflamed as if it had been touched by a hot iron.

"Hey tough guy," the gang leader snarled, "You finished your little speech now? Can we move on?" His eyes flashed angrily. "I think you should prepare yourself, kid," he said looking over the stranger's shoulder toward Jason, "I'm about to blow your boyfriend's head off. Once I'm done with him, I'm coming for you."

He pulled the trigger. A bullet slammed into the stranger's chest. The guy didn't move.

"What the fuck?" the gang leader muttered, his face a mask of shock. He pulled the trigger a couple more times. The gunfire echoed and bounced off the walls as the bullets slammed into the stranger's body but still, he remained standing. "What the hell are you?" the gang leader croaked, unable to comprehend what was happening.

"I'm your worst nightmare," the stranger grinned. His would-be assassin's eyes widened as his flesh began to ripple beneath his jacket. One by one the bullets dropped from his skin onto the floor.

Before the badly shaken shooter had time to fire off another round the stranger had stepped forward. As the gang leader's finger began to curl around the trigger again, the stranger raised his right hand and grabbed the barrel. The gun began to melt. The heat spread up through the rest of the weapon and into the shooter's arm. He dropped to the floor howling in pain as his arm began to burn and fall away. Within seconds it had disappeared as if it had been dipped in acid. All that remained was a bloody blackened stump where the shoulder should have been.

The remaining gang members stared in horror as their leader rolled on the floor screaming. The bald guy acting more out of fear than instinct stepped forward and began swinging his knife at the stranger's head. As the blade swung in toward his face, the asphalt began to burn beneath the bald guy's feet. The fire swept up through his body turning him into a human fireball.

The third guy tried to run. He never made it. The ground around him softened into liquid mud. He started to sink, screaming in terror, thrashing and clawing at the air as his body sank further into the ground. Soon only his head was visible. Just as he looked as if he might drown, the ground hardened again crushing his body like a vice. Blood spurted out of his open mouth onto the floor as he took his last painful breath. As the light went out in his eyes, the stranger stepped toward the gang leader who still rolled on the floor.

"You did this to yourself," he whispered crouching down beside him. "I gave you the chance to live but you didn't take it. Now you will meet your friends in hell."

Grabbing the injured man's head between his palms he stared into his eyes and whispered something that Jason couldn't make out. The gang leader screamed. Though the screaming lasted only seconds it was the most terrifying sound that Jason had ever heard. The sound curdled the blood in his veins and filled him with a dread the like of which he'd never known. When the guy was finally silent the stranger picked himself up from the floor. "You may leave now," he said turning and looking into Jason's eyes.

Jason slowly shuffled toward him. When he was within a couple of feet the stranger stopped him.

"You have twenty-four hours. Say goodbye

to all that you know. When the clock reaches eleven tomorrow night, your debt to me must be paid. You understand what this means?"

Jason's mouth opened and closed like a fish trapped out of water. "Are you going to kill me too?" he blurted out.

"You wear my mark. Your time on this earth is almost at an end. Nothing is for free; you knew that when you agreed to my terms."

"I didn't think that I was going to have to die. Why save me if you intend to kill me anyway?"

"Your soul is pure. It cannot be taken; it had to be given freely. Go now, enjoy the time you have left. You have but hours to make peace with the ones you love."

Jason ran. He sprinted out into the street and away from the nightmare behind him. He kept on running until he'd reached his mother's apartment. The air burned in his lungs as he jumped the stairs two at a time. Making his way up to the fourth floor, he burst through his front door, his body sweaty and exhausted.

"You got my whisky baby?" his mother asked looking up from the couch as made his way into the lounge.

Tears rolled from Jason's eyes. He pulled

the unbroken bottle from his jacket and handed it to her. "I love you ma," he said staring down at her pale face. "But you have to stop doing this to yourself."

His mother didn't answer. She grunted something illegible then snatched the bottle from his outstretched hand. Removing the lid, she lifted the bottle to her mouth and suckled greedily at the lifesaving liquid.

Jason left her and went to his room. Dropping onto his bed he curled up into a ball and sobbed. As the tears fell in steady streams onto the covers, he thought of the life he was about to lose. It wasn't a perfect life, but it was his and he wasn't ready to give it up, not yet. How could he? How could he leave his mother alone? How would she cope without her seventeen-year-old son? After losing her husband prematurely in a work-related accident, he was all she had left.

Determined not to let his mother see him cry, Jason wiped away the tears and sat up. Swinging his legs over the side of the bed he scratched at the red mark on his hand. His skin itched and burned. The mark had blistered. It looked a darker red than before with white blotches around the edges. As he stared at it, his mind drifted back to the ally and the horrific scene that had unfolded. Who the hell was the man that had saved him? Where had he come from? Why did he want to kill Jason? There had to be a way to save himself. The stranger had given him twenty-four hours. He'd already wasted an hour. It was time to pull himself together and figure out what to do.

Leaving the bedroom, Jason made his way back into the lounge. His mother already looked better. The whisky had eased her discomfort a little. She was no longer shaking.

"You been crying baby?" she asked, looking up at him from the couch. What's wrong?"

"It's nothing," Jason lied.

His mother grabbed him. "You lying to me? I heard you sobbing. Are you in some kind of trouble?"

Jason wanted to tell her the truth., but how could he? How could she possibly believe him? He was suddenly angry. He wanted to scream at her that it was her fault, that if he hadn't been fetching her damned drink his life wouldn't be on the edge. Instead, he shook his head and said nothing.

"If you're in trouble, you should go to the police," his mother mumbled. She stared at him through sunken bloodshot red eyes. "I already lost your father; I can't lose you too. Go and fix the problem baby."

Jason clenched his fists. His heart raced in his chest. How could she not know that she was the problem, that everything bad in his life was because of her? the drinking was killing her, and now it looked as if it was going to kill him too. He gritted his teeth to prevent himself from yelling at her and counted to ten in his head.

"You're right mother," he said finally, his voice barely above a whisper. "I am in trouble, but I'll sort it. I want you to promise me though that you'll sort your problem too. You must give up the booze. He's not coming back. You have to deal with that. You need to start living again.

"How dare you?" his mother screamed. She jumped up from the couch and grabbed Jason by his collar. "Never speak of your father that way again. Get out of my house and don't come back until you can show some respect."

Jason removed her hand from his clothing and marched toward the door. "Please mother," he begged. "I love you, but I can't live like this anymore." He opened the door and hovered by the stairwell. "I'll come back later once you've calmed down."

"GET OUT, GET OUT!" he heard her shout behind him as he closed the door and headed toward the stairs.

***

The police precinct was a twenty-minute walk from Jason's apartment. Keeping his head low, avoiding eye contact with the other pedestrians walking the pavement, he headed toward it. Climbing the three steps to the glass doors, he entered the reception foyer and strolled toward the front desk.

"Can I help you?" A burly-looking officer said, looking up from his paperwork as the teenager approached the counter.

"I want to report a murder," Jason replied.

"What's your name kid?" the officer said a suspicious look on his face. "I'm already having a bad night. For your sake, you'd better not be lying to me."

"My name is Jason Ruiz, and no, I'm not lying," Jason, insisted. "Three guys died this evening and I saw it all."

"Ok, where did this triple homicide occur?"

"In an alleyway between a convenience store

and a takeaway."

"Street name son, what's the street name?"

"Oh, it's East 47th," Jason replied.

The officer picked up his radio. "This is dispatch," he said, talking into the mouthpiece. "Any units near East 47th? We have a possible 10-10. Can somebody check it out, over?"

"This is twelve responding. I'm close to that location. I'll go take a look over."

"Thank you, unit, twelve. Let me know what you find."

"Roger that. Twelve out."

"Might as well go sit down," the police officer said indicating toward a bench near the window. Could take a while."

Jason nodded. "Thank you, Mr. Rodriguez," he said reading the name on the officer's shirt.

Fifteen minutes passed. The police radio crackled into life. "Dispatch, this is unit twelve. Have checked out the location, nothing here, over."

"You sure?" Rodriguez responded.

"Affirmative. We've checked the place over and spoken to one or two of the property owners, nobody saw anything. There are no signs to indicate a struggle occurred anywhere in this vicinity.

You sure this is the right location, over?"

Rodriguez looked over at Jason. Jason nodded. "Affirmative," the officer replied.

"Ok dispatch. 10-98."

"Roger that. Dispatch out."

"As you heard," Rodriguez said shaking his head, "They found nothing. Get out of here and don't bother me again. If you do I'll charge you for wasting police time."

"But I'm telling the truth," Jason growled.

Rodriguez shot him a look that said, "don't mess with me."

Realizing that it was useless protesting any further Jason headed toward the door.

Shuffling out of the police station, his hands in his pockets, Jason descended onto the street cold and dejected. What the hell was he to do now? If the police couldn't help him, what chance did he have? His mother needed him. He had to come up with a plan to save himself and fast. If he didn't his death would push her over the edge. The thought was unbearable.

An idea suddenly struck him. Mr. Sanchez, the guy who owned the store he'd bought the whisky from might have some CCTV footage of the gang hanging around outside his building. If

Jason could convince him to hand it over, there might still be a chance. It would prove the gang intended to hurt him if nothing else. If the police saw the footage and investigated further, other witnesses who'd been too frightened to talk might come forward. It was worth a shot.

Picking up his pace, he headed back to the store, hoping that the owners didn't refuse him. Mr. Sanchez was no longer behind the counter when he arrived. Instead, his wife was serving.

"Hello Jason," she said as he made his way toward the counter. "You've already visited us tonight. You missing us already?"

"Something like that," Jason muttered. "Truth is I have a bit of problem. I was wondering if you could help me fix it, Mrs. Sanchez?"

"I'll do my best. So, what is this problem, Jason?"

"When I came in earlier tonight, something happened in the street as I left. I was hoping your camera might have picked it up."

Mrs. Sanchez stared at him. Her eyes narrowed. She didn't look happy. "You're the person who called the police aren't you?" she sighed.

"Yes," Jason replied. "But I had to. There was a gang outside your building. They tried to mug me."

"I'm sorry that happened to you, but I'm afraid I can't help."

"Can't or won't?" Jason responded.

"Look you're a good kid Jason," Sanchez said softly. "I know what you do for your mother. But calling the police? That was a bad thing to do. You could have gotten me into a lot of trouble. I'm breaking the law serving you. You are underage. If the police come in here sniffing around, I could lose my license. You do understand what I'm trying to say?"

Jason nodded. "You've been good to me Mrs. Sanchez. I don't want to cause you any trouble. I won't ask again."

"Good. I'm glad we are on the same page. I'm sorry I can't help you, but at least you're not hurt. Brush it off, be grateful that you are ok."

Jason reluctantly left the store. Zipping the collar of his jacket tight around his neck, he trudged back out into the street. As he began the slow walk back to his apartment he stopped in his tracks. Looming out of the darkness close to the road was a church. In the darkness he'd missed which was hardly surprising. The church wasn't a conventional church at all. It had no big, pointed roof or any of those bright colorful windows that most religious buildings had. It looked more like an office. The only thing that made it stand out amongst the other structures around it was the notice board outside advertising Sunday prayers and the name above the wooden door. "The holy church of St David," the sign read. "Those who open their hearts to the lord shall find everlasting love."

Could they help? he wondered. He had seen the movies. He'd watched the stories of priests casting out demons from the bodies of men and women that had been possessed. Most of the priests in the films had been roman catholic but was that important? Did it really matter what religion the clergyman represented? But what if none of it was real? It was Hollywood after all. Even so, the writers of the films had to get their ideas from somewhere, didn't they? They'd have to of done some kind of research. There was usually some element of truth behind every fictional character. After what Jason had seen tonight, he knew that to be true.

Stepping out of the street, Jason made his way down the small path and tried the door. To his relief, it wasn't locked. The church was open.

New York did operate a twenty-four-hour poli-
cy it seemed. Pushing the door wide he tiptoed
inside, only to find the place devoid of human
activity. Ahead of him, around thirty wooden
chairs were laid out neatly in straight lines with a
small isle running between them. The seats were
all empty. In front of the chairs was a small stage
with a large metal cross attached to the wall and
a wooden pulpit just off-center. The lights on the
low ceiling were all switched on and soft music
was coming from somewhere, but the building
was otherwise eerily quiet.

As Jason ventured further, he noticed a door
close to the stage. Turning right he made his way
toward it. Turning the brass handle he stepped
through the aperture and found himself in a small
room. Directly in front of him was a wooden table. Sitting at the table with his back toward the
door was the priest. On hearing footsteps behind
him, the clergyman turned his head.

"Hello father," Jason mumbled. "I'm sorry
to disturb you at this late hour. I was wondering
if you could spare me a moment of your time. It
is important."

"It must be," the priest replied looking down
at his watch. "It's almost two. You are lucky you

caught me. I was preparing to leave fairly soon."

Jason shuffled awkwardly in the doorway unsure whether to stay or turn around and leave. He was starting to wonder if he'd made a mistake.

"Are you in some kind of trouble?" the priest asked. He was younger than Jason had expected, maybe mid to late thirties. He had a kind enough face, but he was staring at his guest with a look that was somewhere between curiosity and mild annoyance.

Jason nodded.

"I guessed as much. So how can I assist you... sorry I didn't get your name?"

"Oh, sorry It's Jason Ruiz," Jason apologized.

"And I am Father Frank Hill," Frank replied. So, what is the nature of your problem Jason?"

Jason hesitated.

"It's ok. There is nobody here. Whatever you say to me will stay between us and God."

"Ok," Jason replied. But I'm not sure you'll believe me. I'm still trying to get my own head around it. what I'm about to tell you is going to sound crazy."

"Go ahead. I doubt you can surprise me, Jason. In my job, I've seen the very best and the very worst of human nature. I've seen the dregs of humanity. I've heard just about every evil secret that man holds deep within his heart," Hill sighed. "Try me."

Jason cleared his throat "I'm being hunted," he said blurting the words out. "There is a demon chasing me. I've been given twenty-four hours to live. After that, I'm going to die."

"I see," Father hill replied. "And you actually believe this don't you?"

"Yes, I do. I'm frightened father. Can you help me?"

Hill was frowning deeply. "My child, how can I put this?" he said. "Whatever you've done, whatever crime you have committed, if you repent, if you seek the lord's forgiveness, this demon will disappear. He is a figment of your imagination, something you have conjured up to punish yourself. You're not going to die, not tonight anyway, but you must accept responsibility for whatever wrong you have inflicted."

"You don't get it. I haven't done anything wrong. This thing is coming for me because it wants my soul. I was nearly killed tonight by a street gang. A guy stepped in to save me, at least

I thought he was a guy at the time. But he wasn't human. He left his mark on my hand. He told me that I have to repay a debt for his saving me. Look, look at my skin," Jason yelled. He stretched out his hand so that Father Hill could see it. "That is the mark of the devil, isn't it? Am I making this up? This thing is coming for me and I'm running out of time. Please, I beg you, you have to help me."

Hill looked at Jason's hand. "You are even more troubled than I thought," he said shaking his head and tutting. "Why would you do such a thing to yourself? Are you on drugs? Is that what this is?"

Jason clenched his teeth in frustration. "No, I'm not on drugs. If you don't believe me, check my eyes."

Father Hill wasn't listening. He'd already made up his mind.

"I can help you with your problem if you'll let me," he said. "I know a lady; she runs a clinic. It's a place where teenagers with drug-related issues like yourself can go for help. She's very good. I'll give you, her card. You should call her."

"Are you even listening to me?" Jason snapped. "Have you heard anything I've told you? You call yourself a man of the cloth, but do you even believe that your God is real? I bet this church is nothing more than a job to you. I bet you have no faith. All those people you preach your lies to, do they know what you are?"

"Of course, I believe," Hill replied, "and insulting me won't make your problems go away."

"That demon is out there. It exists. It will find me. Why won't you help me?" Jason pleaded.

"Demons aren't real," Hill sighed. "Yes, there is evil in the world, but it is an evil of man's own making. It is born out of his own dark heart. Lust, greed, envy... these are the true evils. There are no monsters with horns out there. They don't exist. And even if they did, there is certainly not one chasing you. Go home, sleep it off. Whatever you've taken is messing with your head. If you still believe this ridiculous story in the morning, come see me again and we'll work together to figure out what is causing your pain."

"Fuck you," Jason said turning and heading toward the door, "I've wasted my time here. You clearly can't help."

When Jason stepped back out into the cold it was getting close to three. The temperature had dropped considerably. Jason shivered beneath the blanket of stars that shone like dull lights above the skyscrapers that swathed the city. Frightened and cold, he headed back to his mother's apartment, no longer caring what happened to him along the way.

The apartment was quiet. Mrs. Ruiz had already slipped off to her room. A half-empty bottle of whisky sat on the kitchen unit where she'd left it. "Why not?" Jason muttered reaching up to the cupboard above and taking out a glass. He'd never touched alcohol before. He'd never wanted to. Having watched his mother drink herself half to death, he'd vowed never to touch the stuff. Tonight, though he no longer cared. He was going to die anyway, so what did it matter.

Pouring the whisky into the glass, he sat on the couch and knocked it back. The whisky was foul. It tasted horrible and it burnt his throat. Coughing and spluttering, he put the glass down and searched for some beers. He found a twelve-pack in the fridge. Only three were missing. Removing the remaining cans, he headed toward his room and began to slurp them down. The beer tasted better than the whisky but only just. but having never touched a beer before it didn't take long before he'd reached a drunken state.

As he Leaned back against his pillow, the room began to swim. Jason sat up fighting against the urge to vomit. It was useless, bile rose in his throat, and he had to run to the bathroom to prevent himself from spewing over the carpet. Hanging his head over the toilet he reached again and again. When there was nothing, but his stomach lining left, he grabbed a glass of water and staggered back to his bedroom. Within minutes he'd drifted off to sleep.

"Hey baby, wake up," his mother was saying. She shook him again as he began to stir.

Jason opened his eyes. He felt like shit. "What time is it?" he mumbled, wiping dried sleep from the corner of his eyes.

"It's three-thirty. You've been sleeping most of the day. I've set you up a baby-sitting job with Julie down the hall so that you can pay me back for those beers you stole from me." She mumbled. "Julie has already given me the money, so don't think you can hide it from me. I don't know what possessed you to drink and I don't care, but you don't ever take my property without asking again you hear?"

Jason nodded. The movement hurt. His

head felt like a freight train was running through it.

"Julie's expecting you at six. Make sure you are there," his mother said turning and leaving the room.

Jason was suddenly wide awake. The memory of the night before hit him like a sledgehammer. He only had seven and a half hours left before the demon came for him. How could he have been so stupid, what had possessed him to turn to alcohol to solve his problems? He'd wasted a lot of time. He didn't have much left.

Leaping from the bed he showered, got dressed, and sprinted into the kitchen. Grabbing some pain killers from the cupboard, he wolfed them down, collected his coat, and ran from the apartment.

"You make sure you are back here for six," he heard his mother shout behind him as he slammed the door and headed for the stairs.

A few blocks from the apartment, hidden away from the street was a communal garden and play area. It was run down and in a bad state of repair. Most of the swings were broken. There was graffiti almost everywhere. The garden was almost completely overrun with weeds. Where paving was still visible, needles littered the ground, left by the addicts that used the place to jack up out of sight of prying eyes.

When Jason reached the park, it was empty. Making his way over to one of the broken swings, he sat down and squinted against the low November sun. "Come on," he muttered, "Think." There had to be something he could do. There had to be some way out of his predicament. Maybe he could reason with the stranger, make a deal with him?

"I know you are watching me," he yelled, hoping that the stranger could hear him. "Come out, show yourself. I want to talk."

He heard rustling behind him, turned, and saw the stranger standing in the shadows next to a broken seesaw.

"What do you want Jason?" the demon asked. "Why have you called me here?"

"This contract, I want to know if there is a way out of it?" Jason replied.

"The contract is binding. It cannot be undone. You are wasting precious time. Go, make the most of what you have left."

"No, I can't accept that. All contracts have clauses. There has to be one in yours."

The only way for you to escape your fate is to get another to take your place."

"So, if I can give you someone else, you'll let me go?"

"Their soul must be pure, alike for alike," the demon responded. "You will not find anyone Jason. Accept your fate. Come to me willingly. You know you have no choice."

"I'll find someone. I still have nearly eight hours."

"Good luck," the demon responded vanishing into the air like smoke.

Jason left the park. He ambled along the street, thinking hard, trying to count the people that he knew. There weren't many. Those that he did know certainly weren't pure of heart. Even if he could find somebody, how the hell would he get them to give themselves willingly? The stranger was right. It was useless. There was no hope. He was damned. It was just a matter of time.

Finally accepting of the fact that all was lost, he headed home. If these were to be his last few hours, he'd have to make them mean something. It was time to make peace with his mother. It was time to say goodbye. She wasn't perfect, she never had been, but she was the only family he had and despite everything, he loved her.

Mrs. Ruiz was on the couch when he walked into the apartment. Nowadays it seemed she never moved away from it. She was already inebriated. She stared at him through puffy bloodshot eyes as he walked through the door. "Hi baby," she mumbled. "You been to see Julie yet?"

"Not yet," Jason replied, "But it's still early. "Right now, I want to talk to you."

"What about?"

"You know I love you, don't you?"

"Of course, I do. I love you too."

"If anything happens to me, I just wanted you to know I cared. That's all," Jason muttered.

"Nothing's going to happen to you silly," Mrs. Ruiz laughed.

"I know," Jason lied. "Hey, let's watch a movie," he said sidling up next to her. "Anything good on the tv? I want to spend some time with you, just like the old days."

"I'd like that," his mother replied. She handed him the remote. "No western's ok, I hate westerns."

"Agreed."

Jason flicked through the channels and found an old musical. "How's this?" he asked.

"Perfect."

His ma was asleep before the movie was a quarter way through. As she lay snoring on the sofa, Jason held her in his arms and cried. At five minutes before six, he got up left the apartment. Crossing the hall, he knocked on Julie Braymer's door and waited. Julie opened the door. She stared out at the blonde teenager and grinned. "Dead on time," she said, opening the door wider to allow him through.

"Jessika has eaten. So, you don't need to worry about feeding her," she said leading him down the corridor to the front room. "There are games on the tv she can play, or she has her tablet if you are bored and want to watch something on your own. There's food in the fridge if you get hungry. You can take her out if you don't want to stay in the apartment, but please don't go far and be back before it gets dark. I'll be home at ten, so you won't have to put up with her for too long. Thank you so much for this Jason. I appreciate you helping me out."

"You are very welcome," Jason replied. He waited for her to leave then looked down at the six-year-old girl and smiled. "What do you want to do," he asked.

"Games."

"Games it is then," Jason grinned. He switched on the tv, let her pick the games she wanted, and then plugged in the controls. For the next hour, they played Mario and some weird building block game he'd never seen before. At 8 pm they had a short break for ice cream. At eight-forty-five he switched off the tv and read Jessika some stories.

"Are fairies real?" she asked in her cute little voice as he read her a tale about Peter Pan and Tinkerbell.

"Of course, they are," he laughed. "You know you can't ever let a fairy know that you're not sure. They rely on us to keep them alive. For every one of us that says they don't believe, a fairy dies."

"I believe," Jessika said looking up at his face," I honestly do."

Jason stared at her. "Well, that's a relief," he said. A thought suddenly came into his head. His heart hammered in his chest. He hated himself for what he was thinking, but the instinct to survive the night completely overwhelmed him.

"Do you want to go on an adventure?" he asked, closing the book, and getting to his feet.

"What sort of adventure?"

"What if I were to take you to a guy who could show you some real fairies, would you like that?"

"Yes, yes, I want to see some fairies," Jessika said excitedly.

"Ok, let's go grab your coat."

Jessika's face changed. "You sure we won't get into trouble?" she asked. "It's nearly bedtime. Mummy gets cross if I stay up late."

"Well, mummy isn't here. She won't be back for another hour. I promise I'll get you back and to bed before she gets here."

"Ok," Jessika responded.

Jason helped her into her coat. He picked out her favourite hat and some gloves and then led her out of the apartment. As they made their way awkwardly down the stairs, Jason sneaked a look at his watch. Ten minutes past nine, one hour and fifty minutes to get her to the demon and save himself.

Central Park wasn't too far away. He figured that even with Jessika's little legs, they could make it in around thirty minutes, still plenty of time to make the swap. If Julie didn't get home early and nobody got suspicious of what he was doing out walking the streets with a child in tow at such a late hour, he'd be able to summon up the demon and make the exchange. What happened after that he'd have to work out later. When it was all over, he'd give Julie some bullshit story that Jessika had walked out whilst he wasn't looking, that he'd searched everywhere but couldn't find her. Mrs. Braymer would be grief-stricken and angry, but she'd believe him, why wouldn't she? He was a good kid and she'd always trusted him, why would that change?

Walking the streets at night and trying to keep a six-year-old occupied was hard work, much harder than expected. She was tired and her tiredness was making her grumpy.

"I want to go home," she yelled as they entered the park. "I don't want to see fairies anymore."

"Oh, come on Jessika," Jason said trying to calm her. "We are almost there now. Are you sure you want to go back? Wouldn't you like to meet Tinkerbell?"

Jessika raised her head. "Your friend knows Tinkerbell?" she whispered wide-eyed and full of wonder."

"He certainly does." Jason lied. "But we

have to get going. He's waiting for us. Can you hold on a little longer?"

Jessika nodded. She held his hand tightly and smiled."

"Good girl," Jason mumbled. He looked at his watch again. It had already turned ten. The journey had taken a lot longer than he'd expected. Julie would already be home and wondering where he was.

His phone rang. He ignored it and carried on walking. A couple of runners jogged past him. They looked at him and then at the girl. Jason could see by the expressions on their faces that they were suspicious of him.

"Come on," he said dragging Jessika along. One of the runners looked back. Jason tried to act like nothing was wrong. It seemed to work. Thankfully neither man stopped.

Ahead was a crop of trees. Making sure that runners had gone and that nobody else was around, Jason led Jessika off the path toward them. His phone rang again. He let it go to voice-mail.

"Is that mummy?" Jessika asked.

"No, it's my friend wondering where we are. Come on, we shouldn't keep him waiting."

The phone rang again. Jason let it ring. In the distance, he thought he could hear the sound of police sirens. "Ok stand there," he told Jessika, trying hard not to panic. "I'm going to call my friend now."

Jessika nodded her head and yawned barely able to keep awake. She stood quietly and watched him as he summoned his friend.

"I bought you this girl," Jason said when the stranger appeared. "I want to make an exchange, her life for mine."

"She is certainly pure. Did she come here willingly?"

"Yes."

"You tricked her." the stranger said.

"Yeah, just like you tricked me. Do you want her or not?"

The stranger stared at the little girl then back at the teenager. "Make your peace with her Jason if this is truly what you desire. But once she wears my mark, know that it cannot be undone."

"Are we going to see Tinkerbell now?" Jessika squeaked.

As Jason looked down into her tiny little eyes, he knew that he couldn't go through with his plan. Crouching down beside her he whispered. "I'm sorry kid. I'm afraid we can't meet her today after all."

Jessika's eyes whelmed up and she started to cry. "It's' coz I said I didn't believe isn't it," she sniffed.

"Of course, not darling," Jason replied. "She's just very busy today that's all."

A few meters beyond the bushes Jason heard voices and running footsteps. The trees were suddenly lit up by the light. A torch shone in Jason's face. It was the two joggers. They had returned and they had bought company. Jason stared at the police officer holding the torch, then at his partner who was pointing a gun straight at Jason's chest.

"Hand over the girl," the officer ordered.

"Don't shoot," Jason pleaded. "I haven't hurt her. She's ok. I'll give her to you." He pushed Jessika away. "Go on," he whispered. "Go to the nice policeman. I've done a bad thing. I shouldn't have brought you here. I'm sorry."

As Jessika ran over to the officers, Jason took off. One of the policemen chased him. He was fast. He caught up with the teenager quickly and bundled him forcefully to the ground. As Jason struggled with him in the mud, the two runners caught up. Seeing the fight in front of them, they jumped in and helped the policeman restrain him. "Give it up son," the officer panted, as Jason was pinned down, "It's over."

"Please," Jason cried. "I'm not a bad man. I had to do it. He made me. I didn't have a choice."

"If was someone helping you," the officer snarled, "You'd better tell me who he is."

"The guy over there by the bush," Jason said twisting his head to look at the stranger.

"What the hell are you talking about?" the policeman replied. "There's nobody there."

"Christ he's standing right next to you," Jason panted, "the guy in the suit. Why can't you see him?"

"Stop with nonsense," the officer replied snapping a pair of handcuffs onto his wrists. "Playing the crazy card is not going to help you tonight."

Outside the park, other police units had already arrived. The whole street seemed to be full of blue flashing lights. As Jason was pushed toward a parked cruiser, Julie Braymer scrambled out of one of the vehicles parked a few feet away. Her face was pale, her eyes were puffy from the tears she'd been crying. "Where is she? What did you do to her you monster?" she screamed at him.

"It's ok. She's safe," one of the officers assured her, gently guiding her over to her child.

Julie scooped her daughter in her arms and sobbed. "Oh darling," she cried. "Thank God. I thought I'd lost you." Turning her head, she stared past her daughter toward Jason's side window. "I trusted you," she mouthed. "Why?"

"You'd never understand," Jason, mouthed back.

As the police cruiser pulled away from the curb, he hung his head in shame.

***

The journey to the precinct seemed to take forever. The police cruiser and its escort following close behind seemed to take a never-ending series of turns. As they drove, Jason became increasingly restless. "What time is it?" he asked.

"Be quiet," the driver replied.

"What fucking time is it," Jason repeated. "I need to know."

"It's one minute to eleven, dickhead," The officer growled. "Now close your mouth or I'll close it for you."

"I have to get out of here," Jason protested. "He's coming for me." He smashed his elbow against the glass, trying to force his way out of the car.

Hearing the commotion coming from the rear seat the driver pulled over to the side of the road. Unbuckling his belt, he made his way to the back of the vehicle with his partner following close behind. "Right, that's it scum bag," he snapped. "Don't say I didn't warn you." He opened the door and his mouth dropped. "What the...?" he muttered. Lying on the back seat, his face twisted into a mask of pure terror was the dead teenager. His mouth was wide open as if caught in one final deadly scream.

The officer scratched his head and looked at his partner. "What the hell just happened here?" he croaked.

"Heart attack most likely," his partner whispered.

On the paving a few feet away from the car, Jason was watching the two officers. Looking down at his body lying on the pavement, he watched the two policemen's desperate attempts at CPR. "I'm dead, aren't I?" he said turning to the stranger. "What happens to me now?"

Feeling a presence behind him, he wheeled around. Two black shadows had risen from the ground. Although the shadows had almost no form, Jason thought that he could just make out dark skeletal demonic faces lurking within. He screamed in terror as they moved toward him.

"Goodbye Jason," the stranger said as the shadows grabbed him and sucked him down. "The contract has been fulfilled." Stepping off from the pavement the stranger vanished into the night.

THE GIRL ON THE BRIDGE

The drive home from the conference centre in Kent had taken longer than expected. Having been stuck in his car for several hours Mike Samuel's body was feeling it. His back ached and his head felt heavy on his shoulders as he fought against the urge to close his eyes and drift into sleep. Winding down his window and turning up the rock anthem playing on his MP3, he breathed in the cold November air and approached the stone bridge that marked the last leg of his journey home, grateful that he only had a few more miles to complete.

As his front wheels thumped onto the incline and began their assault on the small narrow bridge, he noticed the girl leaning against the low stone wall at the centre. She was wearing a thin yellow summer dress with no cardigan or coat to provide her with any kind of warmth and was hugging herself against the cold.

Turning to face into his headlights, she raised her arm to shield herself from the glare and stared at him with a defiant look in her eyes refusing to move out of his way. What she was doing there and at such an ungodly hour was a complete mystery.

Slowing the car to a crawl, Mike Samuels edged the vehicle toward the girl and stopped a few inches away, careful not to clip her with his front bumper. "You ok?" he asked opening his door and stepping onto the floor. "Can I help you at all? Are you lost or something?"

The girl looked confused for a moment. "I don't know where I am. I don't know how I got here," she replied.

"Well, you shouldn't be out here alone. Can I give you a lift somewhere? I can take you into town if you like. Maybe we can find you a hotel for the night, or I could take you to the police station if you prefer? If something has happened, you need to talk to someone."

"It's ok. It's nothing like that. I'm just lost is all. I get like that sometimes."

"You have a medical condition?"

The girl laughed. "You're sweet."

"Look I can't leave you out here. You'll freeze to death. Let me find you a place to hold up, at least until your memory comes back."

The girl suddenly looked embarrassed. "I have no money," she whispered.

"Then you can stay with me. It has to be better than staying out here in the cold."

The girl nodded. "You are very kind."

"Hey it's nothing," Mike replied. "Come on, climb in. The car is nice and warm. My place isn't far. I have a spare room. You can make yourself comfortable whilst we try to figure out who you are."

The girl moved around to the passenger side of the car and climbed in. Despite his tiredness, Michael turned up the heater. He waited for her to buckle up then put the car into gear.

The drive didn't take long. As he pulled into his driveway, the girl looked out of her side window trying to get her bearings. She studied the street, her eyes darting to and fro, taking in every house, every garden, and every parked car. Where are we?" She asked, turning her head to look at him.

"Well, the street you are in is called The Street; original I know. The village is Higgles-Bottom. The county is Wiltshire. Does any of this ring any bells?"

The girl shook her head. She climbed out of the car. "Nice house. Is it yours?" she asked.

"Yes. I live here with my girlfriend Tamara."

The girl looked flustered. "Will she mind me being here?" she asked. "I don't want to cause you any problems."

"It won't be a problem," Samuel's replied. "She's away at the moment. She's gone off with some of her friends for a hen weekend, she won't be back until tomorrow evening."

"Ok, if you're sure it's ok."

"I'm sure," Michael said turning the key in the front door lock. Once the couple were inside, he indicated toward the front room, "Go sit down. I'll make you a hot drink, then I'll sort out your bed for you."

"Thank you," the girl replied. "I'm sorry I'm

causing you such trouble.

"No trouble at all," Michael responded. He could feel himself blushing. The girl was pretty. As she fixed him with her dark brown eyes, he found it hard to look away. There was something about her, a feeling he couldn't shake. With more than a little effort, he finally broke the connection. "Coffee or tea?" he managed to say,

"Coffee would be great," the girl replied.

Michael made the drinks and returned to the room. When he got there, she was sitting on the couch. "Your girlfriend is beautiful," she said looking over at the blonde girl in the photo on the shelf above the fake fireplace.

"Thank you, yes she is," Michael replied. He handed the girl a mug. "I'm sorry, I forgot to ask, do you take sugar? I didn't put any in your cup. Force of habit I'm afraid. Neither Tamara nor I use it. I'm terrible for forgetting that others might."

"It's fine, I'll take the coffee as it comes."

"Ok, let's talk," Michael said as she sipped at the drink. "What do you remember about tonight? Do you remember anything at all? Do you recall what happened prior to you being on the bridge?"

"No, I'm afraid not. My mind is a complete blank."

"Is this something that's happened before?"

The girl laughed. "No of course not, at least I don't think so."

I noticed that you have no bag. Do you usually carry one?

"I'm not sure. I'm sorry. I'm not much help, am I?"

"Stop apologizing. None of this is your fault. We don't know what's happened to you. You look ok but I'd like to be sure," he said shuffling up beside her. As she put her cup down on the coffee table, he turned her head and gently ran his fingers through her auburn hair looking for blood or bumps in her skin. Her hair was thick. He had to dig his fingers in deep to touch her scalp. Finally, having found nothing he released her.

"You're all clear which is a relief. It does however leave a lot of unanswered questions. I guess a good night's sleep might help us figure it out."

The girl yawned. "I am tired. If you won't be offended, perhaps I'll go to my room now?"

"Of course," Michael replied. He followed

her out through the door and up the stairs. "Your room is this one over here," he said indicating toward her bedroom door.

"I've given you clean sheets and pillows. The bathroom is the room over there on the left. There is an unopened toothbrush still in its packaging in the wall unit that you can have. There are fresh towels in the cupboard," he said pointing at a door halfway down the landing. "I guess that's everything."

"Thank you," she whispered. "Your girlfriend is very lucky to have you. I hope she knows that." Again, she fixed him with that stare that sent shivers of excitement through his body. He fought to control himself.

"Night then," he said slipping into his room, hoping she hadn't noticed.

For the next few hours, Michael tossed and turned but his earlier tiredness had gone. All he could think about was the girl. She'd got into his head. He wanted her and he hated himself for thinking it. Finally, as the sun was beginning to climb from its bed in the East, his eyes closed, and he drifted into sleep.

It was almost ten when he woke. The girl was already downstairs. He could hear her moving about. Climbing from his bed he washed and dressed then made his way down to join her.

"You're awake," the girl called out from the kitchen. "I've made you breakfast. I hope you don't mind."

Michael didn't. He could smell the bacon and eggs drifting through the air. His stomach rumbled.

"Go through to the lounge and I'll bring it through," the girl called out as he hovered by the door."

Michael did as he was told. As he sat down on the sofa, the girl came through holding a tray with a plate of food and a coffee. She was no longer wearing the yellow dress she'd been wearing the night before. Instead, she was wearing a black skirt and a white blouse that belonged to Tamara. The clothes were a good fit. They looked good on her. Even so, Michael wasn't happy.

"I'm sorry," the girl muttered noticing the expression on his face. "I should have asked first but you were still sleeping. My dress was dirty. I didn't think you'd mind."

"It's ok," Michael replied regaining his composure. "It was just a bit of a shock that's all." He watched her as she bent down and placed the tray on the coffee table. She was even prettier than he'd first thought. In the light of day, having had the chance to shower and clean herself up she looked stunning. As he stared at her something hovered at the back of his brain. A memory perhaps? It was crazy, but the whole situation seemed somehow familiar.

"I know this is going to sound strange," he said as she joined him on the couch, "but I almost feel like I know you. Is it possible that we have met before? Do you remember anything yet?"

"Things are starting to come back. Just little things. I remember my name now, it's Aamiya."

"That's good. It's a start. But do you remember why you were at the bridge? Can you recall what you were doing there?"

"That's still foggy, but your girlfriend, I think I know her. I think we are connected somehow. I think I'm supposed to find her. I just don't know why."

"That's crazy," Michael said between mouthfuls of food. "You and I are just two strangers who happened to meet on a bridge. If I hadn't been passing at that precise moment, if I hadn't stopped when I did, we'd probably never have met. The chances of your having met Tamara before must be a million to one."

"And yet coincidences do happen. You just told me that you think that we've met."

"I imagined it. I probably didn't get enough sleep. My mind is playing tricks."

"Was your mind playing tricks last night when you hungered for me? Or a few minutes ago when you watched me walk into this room? I know you felt it, that sexual attraction between us. I know that you are fighting it. I can see you struggle. The truth is that you want me as much as I want you. Tell me you don't, and I'll drop it."

Michael put down his knife and fork. He looked into Aamiya's eyes. It was still there, that feeling, that longing. He tried to resist her, but it was useless. Guilt overwhelmed him but her pull was stronger. Giving in to his lust he ripped off her clothes and took her to the floor. Pushing away from the table with his feet, the couple made love repeatedly until both of them were completely spent.

"I can't believe I did that," Michael said leaning back against the couch and breathing heavily. "What the hell is happening to me?"

"I don't know," Aamiyah panted. "But it felt

right, didn't it?"

Michael looked up at the clock on the wall. "Tamara will be home soon. I don't think you should be here when she arrives. I think you should go figure out what's going on somewhere else."

"You're feeling guilty. I get that. I'll leave I promise, but there is something I need to do first. Will you help me?"

"What did you have in mind?"

"I need to go back to the bridge."

"Ok' I'll take you there, but I have to be back before Tamara gets home."

"Let me clean up and then we'll go. I'll make sure that you are back in time."

Michael nodded.

Aamiyah made her way up to the bathroom. She showered and re-dressed. Before heading back downstairs she crept into Michael's room. Something had come into her head. She wasn't sure why, but she couldn't shut out the over-whelming urge to search the place. Padding across the carpet, careful not to make a sound, she began searching through the cupboards and draws. She found the strange object hidden beneath some lingerie amongst his girlfriend's clothes. It was instantly recognizable. The object was metal. It looked like an old-fashioned zippo lighter only bigger. Something in Aamiya's head told her that she had seen the object before. For a moment she just stared at the lighter trying to figure out why it was bothering her so much. The memory hovered at the back of her mind but stayed frustratingly out of reach.

Slipping the lighter into her skirt pocket, she made her way back downstairs, knowing that whatever it was, the object was important and that she must hide it from Michael.

"Ok let's go," she mumbled. She waited for her host to put on his coat, then followed him out of the house and stood by the passenger door whilst he unlocked the car.

"So, what are you hoping will happen when we get there?" Michael asked as he drove. "You think going back to the bridge will jog your memory?"

"It's something you said earlier," Aamiya replied. "You said I had no bag. What if I did and I dropped it? My bag could be lying by the bridge. If it is there, my purse could be inside. There could be a licence or something else with my address on it."

"Makes sense," Michael agreed. "I guess we'll just have to hope that nobody has already found it." He pushed his foot down harder on the accelerator, a new sense of urgency overcoming him.

They made it to the bridge in good time. Pulling onto a grass verge a few metres away so that other cars could pass safely, Michael climbed from his vehicle. Aamiyah jumped out and joined him. The pair walked over the stone structure but found nothing. "Let's look underneath," Michael suggested making his way down the grass bank to the stream below and waiting for Aamiyah to follow.

Aamiyah spotted the bag almost immediately. It was trapped amongst some mud and reeds close to the water. Bending down she scooped it up and brushed off the loose flakes of dirt that covered one side of the leather. "Found it, she grinned."

"Well don't keep me in suspense," Michael replied, waiting for her to open it and check the contents inside.

Aamiyah unclasped the bag and checked the contents. As she looked down at the lighter sitting beside her purse, a lightbulb clicked inside her head. The confusion that had clouded her mind since the night before lifted and drifted away.

"Well?"

"Nothing," Aamiyah lied, "My purse has gone. Someone has taken it."

"That's a bummer. So, what do we do now?"

"Could you drop me in the town you mentioned? I've taken up enough of your time. I'll figure something out."

"No. I don't want you to do this on your own. There's a café there. Wait for me. Once Tamara is home and settled, I'll come down and meet you."

Aamiya nodded. "Ok," she replied.

The town wasn't far from Michael's house. It didn't take long to get there. "Thank you," Aamiyah said as he pulled up outside the café.

"I'll be back as soon as I can," Michael responded. He turned the car around, gave her one last lingering look, then sped away.

Tamara arrived home at twelve. Michael listened to the sound of her tyres rolling across the gravel as she pulled onto the drive. Turning away from the window, he made his way into the kitchen to make her a drink. "Hi baby," she yelled a minute later as she headed through the door.

"Miss me?"

"Of course," Michael replied. "Good weekend?"

"Yeah, it was great, but I'm exhausted. I'm going to go take a shower then I'll tell you all about it."

As she headed upstairs Michael made himself a coffee and sat back down on the couch. He listened to the sound of the shower as it was turned off and her footsteps heading out of the bathroom and into the bedroom. A few minutes later she came back downstairs in her dressing gown, an angry look in her eyes.

"Who was she?" she snapped.

"Sorry what?"

"Who was the girl you had in this house last night?"

"Ok, before you start thinking the worst, let me explain," Michael stammered. "It's not what you think."

"Isn't it?" Tamara replied. "I leave you alone for one minute and you bring another woman into my home. What should I be thinking?"

"Look it's nothing. Last night when I was coming home from the conference, I saw a girl on the stone bridge by devil's dyke. She looked like she needed my help."

"Who was she?"

"That's the thing. I don't know. She had amnesia. She was just wandering around with no money and no place to stay. I gave her a bed for the night. It was the decent thing to do."

"Really? And was this girl pretty?"

"Yes, she was, but that's not the point."

"Did you know she went through my things?"

"Ah yeah. She borrowed some clothes. Her dress was dirty..." He felt his face reddening. "This doesn't sound good, does it?" he muttered.

"No, it doesn't. Were you even going to tell me about her?"

"Of course."

"She's taken my lighter, Tamara growled. "Did you know that?"

"What this one?" Aamiyah said stepping into the room and holding the lighter in the air.

"How the hell did you get in here?" Michael asked a dumb expression on his face.

"I found your spare key under the flowerpot by your front door," Aamiyah replied. "You really should find a better place to leave it you know; anybody could have taken it."

"Why have you come back?"

"It's a long story. I'll tell it to you, but you'll need to be patient."

Tamara was staring at the lighter. Her face had paled. She looked worried.

"Hello Naomi, or should I call you Tamara now?" Aamiya said watching her from the doorway. "You've changed. Have you been looking after yourself? I swear you've put on weight."

"What's going on here?" Michael said looking back and forth from one girl to the other. "How do you two know each other?"

"Like I said," Aamiya replied, "It's a long story."

"Give me back my property," Tamara snarled. She moved toward the doorway barring her teeth like an angry dog.

"Sit down," Aamiyah said pulling a gun from her bag and pointing it at her.

"Who the hell are you?" Michael stuttered. He was staring in shock at the weapon in her hand. What's going on here?"

"Don't worry, I'll explain everything," Aamiyah responded.

"You were playing me all along, weren't you?" Michael retorted. "I bet you never had amnesia. I bet it was all just part of some sick game."

"Michael please," Aamiya replied. "You mustn't ever think of me like that. I'd never lie to you. There's stuff going on here that you don't understand."

"Then quit talking in riddles and explain it to me."

"It's complicated," Aamiya said.

The brief lack of concentration was all Tamara needed. Sensing an opportunity, she lunged forward. Grabbing her enemy by the arm she punched the back of Aamiya's hand knocking the gun from her grip. As the weapon rolled away, the two girls dropped to the floor kicking and punching.

Michael scooped up the gun. "ENOUGH!" he shouted. The two girls ignored him. They continued to fight, tearing, and clawing at one another like a couple of crazed cats. Michael pointed the gun at the ceiling and fired. In the small room, the bullet sounded like a bomb.

The girls stopped fighting. They rolled away glaring into each other's eyes. Pieces of plaster and wood dropped from the ceiling onto the carpet as they crouched just inches apart sizing each other up.

"Get up," Michael ordered. "I think one of

you should start telling me what's going on here."

"Yes, why don't you tell him, Naomi?" Aamiyah muttered."

"Why do you keep calling her that?"

"Because that's her real name."

"She's lying," Tamara snapped.

"Am I? Are you sure about that?"

"What's with this lighter?" Michael asked, bending to pick it up from where it had fallen. "Why is it so important to both of you?"

"Don't touch that," Tamara hissed.

"Why not, it's just a damned lighter isn't it?"

"No," Aamiyah responded, "It's far more precious than that."

"I don't understand?"

"Of course, you don't. Why would you?"

"So, if it isn't a lighter, what is it?"

"I suppose you could say that it's a transponder of sorts,"

"What's that supposed to mean?"

"Your girlfriend is a time transient," Aamiyah replied "The device you are holding is a portal. Your girlfriend is a wanted fugitive. I've come to take her home."

Michael's eyes widened. "You are completely crazy. What's this really about?"

"You're right, this is crazy. She's crazy." Tamara hissed.

"Am I?" Aamiyah responded.

Michael burst into laughter. "I get it now," he managed to say between fits of giggles. "It's a set up isn't it, Tamara? Aamiyah is one of your hen buddies? This is a wind-up you concocted over the weekend. I can't believe I nearly fell for it.

"It's not a trick," Aamiyah muttered. "Otherwise, why would I be carrying a real gun?"

Michael looked down at the mess on the floor and then up at the hole in the ceiling. He stopped laughing. There was genuine shock in his eyes "Ok," he mouthed, "I'm listening."

"Good."

"Your appearance on that bridge last night... it wasn't a coincidence, was it?"

"No, it wasn't."

"This morning, there was a connection. I felt as if I'd met you before. I had, hadn't I? You've known me all along. Is my name Mike Samuels, or Is that fake too?"

"It is your real name, but you're not the person that you think. Naomi has wiped your memory; she's made you forget."

"Forget what? If this isn't my true identity, then what am I?"

"You are a time traveller just like me. You were sent back in time to apprehend Naomi Bracovitz. We'd tracked her to the year 1965 through a weak signal from her transponder. We knew it might be our only chance to get her before she jumped again. When you stepped through the time portal you never reported back. You disappeared from the grid. We've been searching for you ever since."

"Don't listen to her," Tamara screamed. "She's lying. Don't let her suck you in. She's an assassin sent to kill you. Please, you have to trust me. She's not what she says. She's dangerous Michael."

Michael's head was reeling. He didn't know who to believe.

"Naomi has a number tattooed on her wrist," Aamiyah said taking advantage of his confusion. "The number is 6781. It's her prisoner number. How could I know that if I hadn't been sent to apprehend her?"

"Please," Tamara begged. "Yes, I do have that number on my wrist, and I've never tried to hide it from you. It's not a prisoner number, it's my serial number. I am a member of unit one, an organisation set up to police time. It was me that was sent to find Aamiyah, not the other way around. After we realised that she intended to kill you, I was sent in. I've been protecting you ever since, keeping you safe, waiting for her to return."

"Then our relationship... it was all just one big bloody lie. Is that what you are telling me, Tamara? Just so we are clear."

"No," Tamara replied. "I love you. True it didn't start that way, but I developed feelings. How could I not? Please, you mustn't doubt what we have."

Aamiyah threw her head back and laughed. "You are good Naomi; I'll give you that. But you don't love Michael, you never did. You are incapable of love."

Michael looked like a broken man. He was struggling to take in everything that he was hearing, fighting with himself, his head a huge mass of confusion.

"I want you to think about this morning," Aamiyah said lowering her voice almost to a whisper. "That was real. When you made love to me it felt right, didn't it? You knew my body; you knew what I liked. You knew it because we'd done it before. It felt natural because it always been that way. We are soul mates you and me. You can't fake a thing like that. Look inside your-self. You know I'm speaking the truth."

"You bastard," Tamara snarled. She shook her head in disgust. "You couldn't wait, could you? You fucked that bitch the moment my back was turned. Well, I hope she was worth it."

"SHUT UP! BOTH OF YOU!" Michael yelled. "I need to think." He looked down at the lighter, rolling it over in his hands. "Ok, time to find out the truth" he growled flicking the lid open.

"NO!" both girls shouted together.

A green light shot up toward the ceiling. The centre section of the lighter began to change shape. A digital keyboard with a series of num-bers and strange-looking symbols sprung up from its core.

Tamara sprung forward. Before Michael could react, she'd wrestled the gun out of his hands.

"Close the lid," she ordered, pointing the gun at him.

Michael did as he was told. He snapped the lid down and the light vanished. "I trusted you.

I thought I knew you. How could you do this to me?" He croaked.

"Because I could," Tamara replied.

"So, everything Aamiyah said, it was all true? Did you feel anything for me? Was any of it real?"

"I'm afraid not," Tamara responded. "You were just a convenient place to hide that's all. Christ, you were so boring. Do you know how hard it was to keep up the lies? And your snoring... urgh. Still, it's over now, I don't have to put up with it anymore. Goodbye Michael,"

She said raising the gun.

The bullet hit Michael in the chest. He fell back into the door's wooden framework then dropped to the floor. Aamiyah rushed to his side. Air was rushing from his chest. Blood trickled from his mouth as he fought to breathe.

"Seems you have a dilemma," Tamara said edging toward the couple. "Save your boyfriend or let me go? Your choice Aamiya."

As Aamiyah fought to keep Michael alive, Tamara slipped past her and out of the open doorway.

"You have a sucking chest wound," Aamiyah said crouching beside the stricken man. "I've got to find something to plug it if I don't you won't make it. I have to leave you. Try to stay calm. I'll be back in a minute I promise."

Rushing into the kitchen, she managed to find some tea towels and a roll of black tape. It wasn't much but it was the best she had to work with. Making her way back she discovered that it was already too late. Looking down at her former lover she hung her head and fought back the tears. "I will avenge you," she whispered.

"Oh, I doubt that" the voice rang out behind her. Aamiya whipped her head around. It was Tamara, looming over her with a maniacal look in her eyes. She had never left after all but had been waiting, hiding in the shadows. As Aamiyah tried to get up she fired.

The would-be assassin's aim was slightly off. The bullet grazed the side of Aamiya's head then embedded itself in the wall. As she lay on the carpet with blood trickling from her wound, her enemy smiled. "I win. I always do," she said thinking she'd finished her sparring partner off. putting the gun into her bag she quietly walked away.

***

Mike Samuels had been driving for several hours. His eyes felt heavy and his back ached. Fighting against the urge to close his eyes, he rolled the window down and turned up the rock anthem playing on his MP3. Ahead he could see the stone bridge that crossed Devils Dyke. As he got closer, he realised that a woman was standing close to the edge. Reducing his speed, he pulled closer and brought the vehicle to a stop.

The girl was pretty. She was wearing a yellow summer dress and a blue cardigan. She was shivering against the cold. Shielding her eyes against his headlights with her arm, she waited for him to get out of the car and smiled.

"Are you ok?" Samuels asked, concerned as to what the girl was doing there at such a late hour. "Are you lost?"

"No, I'm not lost," the girl replied.

"Do you know how late it is?

"Yes, I know the time," the girl grinned.

Michael noticed the bump in her dress. "Christ you're pregnant," he whistled. "Let me give you a lift somewhere. You shouldn't be out here all alone, especially in your condition."

"You're right," Aamiya replied. "Thank you.

That would be very kind of you."

"My name is Michael, what's yours?" Michael said as she climbed into the passenger seat beside him.

"My name is Aamiya," the girl replied.

"Nice name," Michael responded. "Have we met somewhere? I feel as if I know you."

"Yes, I think you probably do," the girl whispered.

MIRRORS

Demi Miller woke to the sound of the alarm clock clanging in her ears. Irritated at having been woken she cursed and stretched out her arm to hit the silence button. Rubbing the sleep from her eyes, she tried unsuccessfully to recall the strange dream she'd been having, but it was useless, it had already vanished from her mind like a puff of smoke disappearing into the aether. Rolling out of bed she slipped on her bathrobe and made her way downstairs frustrated and beaten.

As she walked into the kitchen her husband

Eugene looked up from his paper and smiled. He was halfway through a mug of coffee and had already washed and dressed.

"Been awake long?" she enquired pouring herself an orange juice from the fridge and joining him at the table.

"A couple of hours," Eugene replied. "I couldn't sleep."

"Wish I could say the same," Demi sighed. "I was having an amazing dream before that bloody clock woke me. Damned if I can remember what it was about though."

"Goes like that sometimes," Eugene responded. Folding his paper, he glanced at his wife with a playful twinkle in his eye. "Now that you are up, how are you feeling? Big day today. Nervous?"

"Why would I be nervous?" Demi responded, "One school is just like another. Just because we've moved states, it doesn't mean that anything has changed. Kids are kids. Some are good, some are bad. It's always been that way and always will be."

"Oh, come on. Aren't you even the slightest bit nervous?" Eugene teased." I know you like to put on a hard face, but there's a soft-core hidden somewhere underneath that armour-plated shell you like to wear. Despite what you like people to see, just remember, I know the real you."

"Ok, darling. You win. Yes, I do have one or two butterflies flapping around inside me. But you tell anyone I'll have to kill you," she laughed.

Eugene pushed up from his chair. "I have to leave soon," he said, his face becoming a little more serious. "Would you like me to make you some breakfast before I go?"

"Thank you but I'm not hungry," Demi replied, "I'll eat later."

"Ok, make sure you do," Eugene said putting his empty mug into the sink. "Can't afford to have you waste away, can we?" kissing Demi softly on the mouth he left the room to do some last-minute chores.

As her husband clanked around in the next room Demi mentally prepared herself for the day ahead. Pouring herself another juice, she sat back down at the table and ran over her principal's brief in her head.

From what she could make out from the phone calls she'd received; the new high school wasn't all that different from the one she'd recently left. It was smaller than she'd been used to but not by much. There were one or two problem students to be aware of but other than that, there didn't appear to be any major hurdles to overcome. The new job seemed like a good fit. Although she was nervous, she had to admit that she was also a little excited.

Shaken her from her thoughts, Demi looked up as Eugene returned to the kitchen. Giving her one last lingering kiss, he waved goodbye then left the house leaving Demi alone.

Finishing her drink, she made her way upstairs and got undressed. After a quick shower, she picked out an outfit from her closet, got changed, applied her makeup then studied herself in the mirror.

She didn't look too bad for a woman of thirty-two she thought staring at the reflection. Her hair, which had just recently been cut into a bob made her look younger, and the lush brown dye her stylist Julianne had used to cover the odd grey hair that had begun to sprout up looked pretty neat. Overall, she was pleased.

Happy that she looked presentable for her first day at her new school, Demi picked up her briefcase and her car keys, checked to make sure she'd turned everything off, and left the house.

Glemmingdale High School was just a twenty-minute drive from her new home. The school traffic though, made the trip seem a lot longer. Weaving through the many cars that lined the roads, Demi made it to the school gates, flushed and slightly irritable. Pulling into her assigned parking slot within the grounds, she applied her handbrake, sat back, and let out a huge sigh of relief.

Principal Charlene Stohl was already waiting behind her desk when Demi finally made it to her office. She was a large woman with black hair tied in a neat bun and a big round friendly face. Climbing from her chair, she extended a warm clammy hand and greeted her new member of staff with a huge smile before inviting her to join her for a tour of the school's facilities. As Demi tagged along behind her, she moved down the corridors pointing out the various classrooms, the science laboratory, the canteen, and the teacher's restroom. Once she was happy that Demi knew how to find her way around, she led her to her first class.

Demi could already hear the commotion coming from inside the room as she approached the door. The student's voices travelled out into the corridor, an explosion of noise that echoed off the walls as they laughed and joked with one another, waiting for the first lesson of the day to begin.

"Ok everybody, quiet down please," Stohl ordered, opening the door, and stepping inside. Everybody stopped what they were doing apart from three kids who were surrounding and poking a pale, skinny black haired goth girl who seemed to be trapped against her desk in the corner.

"That includes you, Denise Abrahams, vanity Williams, and Jolene Peterson." Stohl bellowed.

The three girls moved away from the desk their faces a mixture of annoyance and defiance. As the principal watched on, they slowly returned to their seats knowing better than to argue.

"This is Demi Miller or Mrs. Miller to you," Stohl said once the three girls were seated. "She is your new history teacher. She will be replacing Mr. Anderson for the rest of the term. Demi has come to us from Alabama. She is highly respected and extremely well qualified. We are very lucky to have her join our team. Please make her feel welcome. Listen to what she says, and you will learn a lot from her I promise."

Right, all yours," she said turning to Demi. "Any problems you know where to find me."

Demi waited for the principal to leave then turned to address the room. "Please take out your books, Apostles of Disunion, and turn to page forty-one," she said. "We will continue our studies where Mr. Anderson left off."

The kids all dug into their bags and placed the opened books onto the table. "Anyone like to start us off?" Demi said once they were all ready to begin. The female student who Demi had seen struggling in the corner stood up and raised her hand. "Ellie Krasz, isn't it?" Demi asked studying her closely and trying to remember the names she'd been given in her brief."

"Yes ma'am," Ellie responded. She paused and gazed at the new teacher, a whimsical look on her face. "You have nice eyes," she purred. "I think she'd like them."

"Sorry, who would like them? You're not making sense."

"She's a nut job," one of the three girls who been picking on Ellie piped up. "Don't let her get into your head. You'll never get her out." Her two friends both burst into laughter.

"That's enough," Demi responded, raising her voice to get above the noise. "I won't have that kind of attitude in my classroom. You and I will have words at the end of this lesson. As for you Ellie, if you have nothing constructive to say, then I suggest you sit down."

Ellie looked wounded. She slid into her seat and stared down at the floor her eyes close to tears. Around her, the room descended into chaos. Once Demi had calmed everyone down and the room was silent once more, she began her lesson.

The rest of the morning was uneventful. Having given Denise Abrahams and her two buddies a quick telling-off at the end of the first period, everything had run smoothly. At Dinner, she met a couple of her fellow teachers in the staffroom. The two men's names were Buck Ralston and Pete Beiler. Both had been at the school for a while and seemed to know everything there was to know about everyone.

"I'm surprised that Stohl managed to get you to come here," Buck said as Demi sat down at the one table in the room and begun tucking into her microwave meal. "I take she told you about the missing students?"

Demi nearly spat out her lasagne. "I'm sorry?" she gasped wiping pasta from her mouth. "What do you mean, what students?"

"Eight students have vanished from campus. The police have not been able to find a single clue as to what happened to them. They think the kids are dead, but as yet no bodies have turned up."

"That's awful," Demi replied. "And no, Mrs. Stohl didn't mention a thing. Do you have any idea what's happening to these kids, do you have a theory as to who's taking them?"

Ralston shook his head and shrugged.

"You've met Ellie Krasz," Beiler said putting down his tea and gazing over at the new teacher, "she's a little odd right? What do you make of her?"

"She's harmless enough."

"Don't be too sure of that. The kid is a complete nut job. So is her boyfriend. I wouldn't be surprised if they are somehow mixed up in all this."

Demi was incredulous. "Surely you're not serious?" she muttered. "I doubt Ellie has a mean bone in her body. Jesus Pete, I'm a little disappointed. I expected a lot better from you. That poor girl has had it hard enough here already. All the kids in her class seem to enjoy picking on her. Don't you think it's your responsibility to provide her with a duty of care? If she can't trust the teachers, what chance does she have?"

Beiler let out a large snort. "I'm sorry, but you've only been here a day. You haven't seen what I've seen. I stand by what I say. The kid should be in a home. She's not right."

Demi threw the remains of her dinner in the trash. "I'm suddenly not hungry," she said turning and leaving the room.

Walking out into the corridor, she headed back to her classroom angry and deflated When she got there Ellie was waiting outside the door. "What are you doing here?" she asked upon seeing the girl. "Shouldn't you be heading off to your next lesson by now?"

Ellie nodded. "Yes, she replied. "But I wanted to thank you. You were kind to me this morning. When those girls picked on me you stopped them. You didn't have to say anything, but you did."

"It's my job. I'd do the same for anyone."

"Well thank you anyway miss," Ellie responded. She looked up at the teacher through heavy black makeup and held her in her gaze. "You helped me so now I'll help you," she whispered. "Don't look in the mirrors, Promise me?"

"What's wrong with the mirrors Ellie?" Demi asked. "What do you mean? Are you ok?"

"I don't want her to find you miss. I can't let her see you," Ellie replied. Before Demi could respond she'd begun walking away.

Shortly before home time, Demi had to run to the staffroom. She'd drank too many coffees during her lunch break and couldn't hold it in any longer. Heading to the lady's toilet she relieved herself then began washing her hands under the faucet. As the water trickled over her skin she thought about Ellie's words. "What a weird girl," she laughed, shaking her head.

As Demi turned off the tap and looked up at the mirror, she saw something in her reflection, a black shadow was moving across the floor behind her. Whirling around she realised that there was nothing there. Shrugging it off as nothing more than her imagination, she left the room.

Leaving the building and heading out to the car park, Demi saw Ellie standing next to her vehicle. "Are you stalking me Ellie?" she asked, wondering what the girl was doing there.

"Someone's damaged your car," Ellie said stepping away so that the teacher could inspect the car.

A huge scratch ran the length of the paintwork. The scratch was deep and stretched from the front wing right back to the trunk. "Did you do this?" Demi snapped.

"No miss," Ellie protested. "Would I be standing here if I'd done that to your vehicle? I'd run, wouldn't I?"

"Well, that would be the most logical reaction," Demi said wanting to believe her. "But as you are the only person around, you can understand why I might have my doubts?"

Ellie nodded but said nothing.

"Well, I think we can get to the bottom of this easy enough," Demi said opening her car door. "I have a dashboard camera. Let's look at the footage, shall we? We'll find the culprit easily enough."

Ellie suddenly looked uncomfortable. "Well, I'll leave you to it, Miss," she said turning to walk away.

"Oh no, not so fast," Demi said stopping her in her tracks. "Unless you have something to hide, we'll look at this together. Stretching across the passenger seat, she reached out and grabbed the recorder. "Ok, let's take a look then, shall we?" she muttered.

"I'm sorry, I'm sorry," Ellie yelled as Demi hit the rewind button. "You don't need to do that. I admit it, I'm the one who scratched your car."

"But why? What reason would you have for doing such a thing? Do you know how much that's going to cost me to repair? What did I do to deserve that?"

"She made me miss," Ellie replied choking back tears. "I couldn't say no. I have to do what she says. I can't fight her, I've tried. She always gets her way. She knows I'm weak and that I need her. She's seen you; she knows you now. There's nothing I can do. She'll mess with you because she thinks it's fun."

"What the hell are you talking about?" Demi replied angrily.

"Milandra, the girl in the mirror," Ellie sniffed.

Demi was quiet for a moment. Switching on the camcorder to make sure that Elle wasn't covering for someone else, she played back the footage then turned it off in disgust.

"Where do you live?" she asked as Ellie

shuffled uncomfortably next to the damaged vehicle.

"On the edge of town, close to the border with Marietta," Ellie replied.

"Ok, get in. We are going to speak to your folks," Demi ordered. "You know I can't let you get away with this don't you?"

Ellie climbed into the car and buckled up. She stared at the teacher with a sad look on her face. "I am sorry," she whispered.

"Ok, tell me where to go," Demi said as they drove through the streets and headed towards her home. Ellie gave her instructions, pointing out roads here and there and telling her to turn left and right. When they were close, she pointed to a road sign that said Hill Street. "That's my road," she said indicating that Demi should turn. "It's number 1422."

Demi pulled up outside and turned off the ignition. Climbing out of the car she followed Ellie up the three steps to the front door then followed her inside.

The house was what was known as a shotgun house. It had four rooms, two on the left and two on the right with a narrow corridor leading through the middle leading straight toward the back door. The houses had gotten their nickname because it was believed that you could fire a shotgun through the front door with a clear path straight through the back of the house.

As Ellie made her way inside, an African woman stepped out of the nearest door on Demi's right.

"Who's your friend Ellie?" she asked staring at the teacher. "You in trouble again?"

Ellie nodded.

"Hi, I'm Demi Miller," Demi said introducing herself, "I'm Ellie's history tutor. I'm looking for her mother. Is she around?"

"You're looking at her," the African woman replied. "My name is Kathleen Johnson, I'm Ellie's step mum. Her real mother left a long time ago. What's your reason for being here Mrs. Miller? What's Ellie done this time?"

"Perhaps we could sit down," Demi replied.

Kathleen Johnson nodded her head and led the teacher into the room she'd just vacated. Taking a seat near the window, she told Ellie to go and fetch some drinks then indicated to Demi to sit on the couch. "Ok, I'm listening," she said, watching the teacher with a guarded expression. "What's she been up to?"

Demi waited for Ellie to return. Once the girl had placed two orange juices in front of the women and sat down with her own, she talked.

"I'm afraid your daughter has vandalized my car," Demi said.

"How bad is this alleged damage?" Kathleen replied.

"It's not alleged, I have camera footage to prove it. As for the damage, it's a large scratch. It runs down one side of my vehicle. Until I get a quote from the garage, I'm not sure how much it is going to cost to repair. Best guess, maybe six or seven hundred dollars?"

"I don't have that kind of money," Kathleen snapped. "You sure it's her on this fancy camera of yours?"

"Yes, I'm afraid so."

Ellie moved across the room and climbed into Kathleen's lap. "I'm sorry," she whimpered.

"It's ok Ellie, Mamma gonna make it better," Kathleen purred. She stroked the teenager's hair and kissed her tenderly on the cheek. Looking over at Demi her face hardened. "Well, you said your piece Missy," she growled. "I'm sorry about your car, but it's done. I can't undo it. I don't know why Ellie took it upon herself to do what she did, but she's apologised. Let that be the end to it."

"That's it? That's all you are going to say. Aren't you going to punish her?"

"Seems to me she's been punished enough," Kathleen spat. "Look at the state you put her in." She pushed her daughter from her lap and sprang from her chair. "We can't pay to fix your car. The way I see it, you can either deal with that, or you can go report her to the police, either way, I want you to leave my house. You are no longer welcome here Mrs. Miller."

Demi was shocked by the aggression in Kathleen's voice. She considered arguing back but the look in the woman's eyes told her that confrontation would end badly. Turning away, she headed for the door and back to her car shaken and bemused.

Eugene was in the lounge when Demi walked through her front door. Throwing herself into his arms, she hugged him and fought back the urge to cry.

"What's wrong?" he asked when she'd finally let him go.

Demi sank onto the couch and recanted the day's events. As her husband poured her a glass of wine and joined her on the couch, she felt the earlier tension begin to ease.

"Ok, it's bad, but it's not the end of the world," Eugene said once she'd finished her story. "We'll call the insurance company in the morning and find out how much it's going to cost us. Then you can go see the principal. It happened on the school grounds. If the two of you put your heads together, I'm sure you can work out a fair punishment. If it were me, I'd probably consider expulsion."

"No. I don't want it to go that far. I think the poor girl just needs a little help. Perhaps I can get Stohl to make her talk to a counsellor. I'm sure we can straighten this out if we try. Ellie's a good kid deep down. I don't want to give up on her over one nasty incident."

"Your choice," Eugene responded. "You're the boss."

The night was filled with bad dreams. Demi woke in the early hours with sweat pouring from her body. Stripping out of her nightdress she showered and returned to her bed and listened to the gentle snores of her sleeping husband. As she lay beside him, she recalled the dream that had woken her.

In the dream, she was being chased through a series of mirrors by a big black shapeless mass. The thing was somehow alive. It homed in on her, sapping her strength, trying to smother her. As she ran from it, she could feel her legs buckle. As she dropped to her knees, it found her, consuming her body inside itself. As the darkness closed around her, she felt the air rushing from her lungs. She struggled to breathe, but her body grew weaker. The mass pushed against her, then poured into her mouth, a black ooze that dripped into her throat drowning out her screams. At the last moment as death seemed inevitable, she woke.

The dream had seemed so real. It had also seemed familiar to her somehow as if she'd dreamt it before. Lying in the darkness, she stared at the ceiling wondering what the dream meant as she counted down the hours 'til dawn.

The next three days were quiet. With Ellie suspended until the following week and with promises that she sees a counsellor upon her return, the days had run smoothly. On Friday morning that all changed. Just before lunch, as Demi was tidying her desk before heading to the staffroom, a breathless Pete Beiler burst into her classroom. "I need to talk to you," he said closing the door behind him. "It's important."

"What's this about?" Demi asked concern etched on her face.

"Ellie's boyfriend Dean Caney has been released," Pete responded.

"I'm sorry, I don't understand?"

"Look I never got tell you the full story about him before," Pete explained. "But he's bad news."

"Why are you telling me this?"

"Sit down, I think you'll need to," Beiler muttered.

"It's ok. I'll stand."

"This guy Dean. He's been in the state penitentiary for the last year. He was incarcerated on drug-related charges. We expected him to be away for longer, but it appears that he's been released early."

"How old is he?" Demi asked, confused that he'd been wallowing inside the state penitentiary." Shouldn't he have been doing his tome inside in a juvenile centre?"

"No. Dean isn't one of our students," Pete replied, "He never was. He's older than Ellie. I'm not sure how they met, and I don't care. What I do know is that he's very protective of her and that makes him dangerous."

"So how much older is he?"

"He's twenty-one, nearly twenty-two I believe."

"Christ, what's Ellie doing with him? She's only just turned fifteen for God's sake. Haven't her parents tried to stop the relationship?"

"Have you met them? Kathleen doesn't seem to give a shit and her husband is never there. He's practically been welcomed to the family with open arms."

"It certainly explains a lot," Demi said thinking aloud. "These drugs he got arrested for, what were they? Does he give them to her?"

"Not sure, but it's very probable. I think you're missing the point here though Demi."

"Which is?"

"You need to watch your back. Caney is seriously bad news. He attacked a pupil a while back, a guy by the name of Reece Sanders. Dean beat him within an inch of his life. Reece was in the hospital for weeks. Caney broke several of his bones and stabbed him. The poor boy had to undergo emergency surgery. He lost a kidney. It was touch and go whether he'd survive."

"And Dean wasn't charged?"

"No, nothing could be proved. Reece wouldn't talk. He was too scared. Caney had some of his bastard friends threaten him. The same guys also gave Dean an alibi. The police had to drop the charges."

"And you think this same man is coming after me?"

"I don't know, but as I said, he's protective. If he's back out and he knows about Ellie's suspension, he might take it personally. I'm just giving you the heads up is all."

When Demi left the building at home time, she was more than a little nervous. If Ellie's boyfriend were as bad as Pete Beiler had implied, it would be smart to keep her wits about her. Heading towards her car she constantly checked around her, but nobody was following. With relief, she climbed into her vehicle and drove home.

At just after midnight Demi and her husband were woken to the sound of the car alarm sounding outside. Rushing out into the street, Eugene noticed that the side window of Demi's car had been smashed. As he got closer, he realised that both the front and back tyres had been slashed and graffiti had been sprayed onto the bonnet. "Die Bitch!" the words read. Eugene looked around searching for the culprit, but he could see nobody. Turning off the car alarm he fumbled for the dashcam, but it was gone.

When the police had arrived, taken statements, and left, the couple returned to their bed.

" Do you think it was him?" Eugene asked as they lay awake unable to sleep.

"I don't know," Demi replied, "but can you think of anybody else that would want to do this to us? I certainly can't."

"Well, I'm damned if I'm going to let him harass you," Eugene growled. "I have a good mind to drive over there and sort him out."

"And what would that achieve? If this guy is as bad as they say, you'll just end up getting hurt. Let the police deal with it. There's nothing we can do for now. Ellie's back at school Tuesday. I'll have words with her then."

When Ellie Krasz entered the classroom on Tuesday morning, she was even more quiet than usual. She went to her seat and sat down refusing to meet Demi's eye. As the lesson progressed, the young teenager kept her eyes down deliberately focusing on her books, refusing to look up.

When the bell sounded, she tried to slip away with the rest of the students. Demi grabbed her as she tried to creep past. "Was it Dean?" she asked angrily."

"Was what Dean?" Ellie replied, an innocent look on her face.

"I had to get my husband to bring me to work this morning," Demi snapped. "You already knew that though, didn't you? So, I'll ask you again, did your boyfriend vandalise my car?"

"I don't know. How am I supposed to know what he gets up to?"

"Why are you acting this way, Ellie? I thought you and I were friends. You told me you liked me for God's sake. Why this change in attitude towards me?"

Ellie stared at the floor and shrugged.

"I guess you and I will have to go and see the principal again," Demi muttered. "If you won't talk to me, then perhaps you'll talk to her."

"Why do you think it was Dean that attacked your car? He doesn't know you. Why would he do something like that?" Ellie said finally meeting Demi's eye. There was something odd in the way she looked at the teacher. Demi couldn't be sure if she was reading it right, but it was almost as if Ellie were trying to tell her something. The moment passed leaving Demi unsure if she'd imagined it.

"Ok. So, if your boyfriend didn't do it, who did? Was it you? It wouldn't be the first time would its Ellie?"

"Maybe you should ask Milandra what happened. I told you not to look in the mirror. You know she's seen you now. You should get away before it's too late."

"Stop!" Demi ordered. "I've had enough of this. There is no such person as Milandra. Let's hear what Stohl has to say about your imaginary friend, shall we? Maybe I should have let her expel you after all."

Principal Stohl looked up from her desk as Demi marched Ellie into her office and closed the door. "Problem," she asked staring at the new teacher.

As Demi explained what had happened the night before Stohl listened intently. She waited until Demi had finished then curled her lip and sighed. "The way I see it, there's nothing we can do," she said bluntly. "This act of vandalism happened off of school grounds. As there are no witnesses to the crime, I can't help. If Ellie or her boyfriend were involved, find me proof. Until then there's nothing I can do. I'm afraid this whole situation is out of my hands."

Demi nodded. The principal was right. There was no proof. She was powerless to act.

"Go to your next lesson," Stohl said addressing the young student. "You're dismissed."

As Ellie slipped away, Stohl turned to Demi. "I know you are angry that this is happening to you," she said softly, "But you really can't go around accusing people without evidence. My suggestion to you is to try to make peace with Ellie. The more you continue to harass her, the worse the situation will get. I don't want this thing spiralling out of control. Are we clear?"

"We're clear," Demi responded.

"Good. Go home. Take the rest of the day off. Go Sort out your affairs. Come back tomorrow when you've calmed down."

Demi did as she was told. After calling her husband to let him know not to pick her up from school as she was going to leave early, she called a taxi and made her way home.

Having watched the taxi pull away behind her, Demi approached her front door and removed the door keys from her purse. As she pushed the key into the lock, she noticed that it was already unlocked. Alarm bells rang in her head. She was fairly sure that she'd locked it when she'd left for work, but could she be certain? With everything going on she could have forgotten.

Hovering on the front step like a frightened child, she began arguing with herself, trying to decide whether to go inside or to call the police. What if someone was waiting inside the house ready to harm her, she wondered.

"Don't be silly," her inner voice told her. "You just forgot to lock it. If you call the police and nobody is in there, they'll start thinking you're a flake."

Fighting against her better judgement, she grabbed the door handle and entered the building.

The house was quiet. Demi breathed more easily. Nobody appeared to be waiting to jump out at her from the shadows Moving from room to room she began checking just to make sure. When she reached her bedroom, her heart jumped in her chest. A man was sitting on her bed. The man was dressed completely in black and wearing a balaclava and thin black gloves. In his right hand, he was holding a knife. Spring-ing from the bed before she had time to run, he grabbed her and put his left hand over her mouth to prevent her from screaming.

"Sit down on the bed," he whispered in her ear. "Don't make a sound or I'll cut you to piec-es. Nod if you understand."

Demi did as she was told. She nodded her head trying desperately to stay calm.

Releasing his hand from her mouth, the man turned her around and pushed her forceful-ly toward the bed.

"What do you want?" Demi stammered once she'd been made to sit. "Are you going to hurt me?"

"Well, that depends on you bitch," The stranger replied.

Demi was shaking badly. Thoughts tumbled through her head like dominoes. What if she never saw her husband again? What if this guy intended to rape her?"

"I know what you're thinking. I know what's going through that pretty head of yours, but I'm not here to hurt you, not yet at least. I just want you to listen to me for a moment. Can you do that?" the man growled.

"Ok," Demi responded. She was breathing deeply, using every ounce of self-control to stop herself from falling apart.

"You and your husband rent this house, or did you buy it?" the intruder asked moving closer. He held the knife in front of Demi's face so that she could see the blade's sharp edge clearly, making sure that she knew he meant business.

"We rented it," Demi croaked. "We wanted to see how things panned out here before we started looking for a place to buy. Is that what this is about? Are you after money?"

"No. it's not about your money darling. I just wanted to get a feel for your situation, that's all."

"Why? I don't understand?"

"Because it will be easier for you to leave if you don't have a mortgage hanging around your neck. That is what this is about. I want you to pack your stuff and go. You're not welcome here. Tell your husband you made a mistake, tell him you have a bad feeling for the place, hell, tell him whatever you like, coz if you don't, I'll come back and next time it won't be just to talk."

"It's not that easy," Demi pleaded. "Eugene has a new job. He won't just pack everything up on my say-so. He has a future here. You can't do this to us.”

“If I were you, I’d stop whining and start thinking about how you are going to change his mind. When I leave this house, I’ll be watching you. You’ll think I’m gone, but I’ll still be in this town, waiting quietly, biding my time, checking to see if you are being a good girl. I can get to you whenever I like, you want to remember that.”

He paused for a moment then stepped back.

“I think we’re done here,” he said running his fingers along the flat of the knife playfully. “I’m leaving now. I want you to count to one hundred before you get up from that bed. If I think you are following me, I’ll come back and I’ll hurt you bad. Believe me, you don’t want that. Remember what I’ve told you. Do the right thing. Pack up and leave whilst you still can.”

Demi was still shaking when she crept downstairs. Her heart thundered in her chest as she moved from room to room making sure that her visitor really had gone. Taking her cell phone from her bag she called the police and then her husband.

***

Eugene arrived home as the police were finishing up with their statements. Having checked the house for fingerprints and come up with nothing, they were getting ready to depart.

"And you say that you think this was Caney?" the officer asked giving Eugene a cursory glance as he slipped past him into the kitchen.

"Yes, I do," Demi replied. "Who else do you think would have a grudge against us? We haven't been here long enough to make any enemies."

The officer put away his notebook. "Ok, we'll go speak to him. I must warn you though Mrs. Miller, I don't hold much hope for you. You didn't see your assailant's face and he's left no fingerprints to prove that he was ever here. I'm afraid he'll probably walk away from this like he always does. The guy is like oil, he's slick. Nothing ever seems to stick to him. He's a bad one, but he's also clever. He's probably been behind half the assaults in this town, but he always seems to wriggle free when we try to put him in a clamp. We'll do what we can, but don't get your hopes up."

"So that's it? He'll just get away with it?" Eugene reacted angrily.

"We questioned your neighbours, nobody

saw anything. Unless you can find someone willing to talk to us, I'm afraid my hands are pretty much tied."

"What if he comes back? My wife was threatened in her own house for God's sake. Can't you get someone to watch over her?" Eugene growled.

"We only have a small department sir, which means we only have limited resources. I can send a squad car past your home now and then if it'll make you feel better, but we don't have the funds available to have anyone sit outside your property twenty-four-seven. Cross your fingers, we might get lucky. If Caney hasn't been quick enough to work his alibi, we might still be able to catch him. He's out on probation so he's on a thin rope."

Eugene rested against the work unit beside the sink trying to control his temper. Demi could see by the look in his eyes that he was close to losing it. Grabbing hold of his hand and squeezing gently she turned to the officer and thanked him for his help. As he walked out through the front porch, she tightened her grip on her husband's hand. "Let it go," she whispered.

When the policeman was safely in his car and had begun pulling away, Demi began locking all the doors and windows in the house. Once she was happy that her home was secure, she poured herself a stiff drink, sat down with her husband on the couch, and waited.

She got the news she'd been expecting three hours later. A police cruiser pulled up outside and a young officer stepped out of the vehicle. Caney had been arrested, he explained as he stood just inside the doorway. Unfortunately, he had provided a sound alibi and would be released within the next hour. After a rather feeble apology, the policeman turned and left.

That night Demi and her husband went to bed early. Having watched a bland evening of tv and knocked back over a bottle and a half of wine to calm their nerves, the couple had rechecked the locks then made their way to the bedroom. Around eleven-thirty Demi slipped into a drink-fuelled sleep, the mixture of alcohol and her own body's defence mechanism finally shutting her down. With her husband still holding her tight in his arms, she drifted into the dark space inside her head where nightmares lurked in every corner waiting to welcome her home.

It was nearly three in the morning when she woke. Sitting up in her bed she craned her ears wondering what had caused her to open her eyes. Eugene was no longer in the bed. Maybe it was the sound of him moving around downstairs that had caused her to awaken. Climbing from the covers, she threw on an old pair of slippers and left the bedroom. Easing her way down the narrow staircase, and holding onto the banister for support, she called out to the silence. The house remained eerily quiet.

When she reached the bottom stair, she noticed that the front door was slightly ajar. Fear rose in her stomach, an unwelcome invader filling her with dread. She fought to push it back, but it seeped through every part of her body clutching her in its icy cold hands.

Staring at the open door she took a deep breath and grabbed the handle. Maybe Eugene was outside she told herself. Maybe he'd been unable to sleep and had decided to take a stroll. It was possible, he'd always been a light sleeper. It wouldn't be the first time he'd gone for a moonlit walk. With everything that had happened the previous afternoon, it would be a reasonable explanation.

Stepping out into the cold she began checking the street, her heart hammering in her chest as she walked back and forth, hoping to see her husband walking towards her with that dopey grin on his face. Instinct told her he wasn't coming, that she'd never see him again. Her fear turned to panic.

Running back into the house, slamming the door behind her, she began searching for her phone. It was on the kitchen unit in her bag where she'd left it. As she removed the phone and lifted it to her ear, she stopped. What would the police think of her if it turned out to be a false alarm? She'd called them several times already, if she called them again, they'd begin to think that she was some weak, pathetic woman with a loose grip on reality. She decided to wait. If Eugene had just gone for a walk, she'd need to give him time to get back.

Deciding that she needed a coffee to calm her nerves, Demi plugged in the coffee machine and flicked the switch. As she reached up into the cupboard for a mug, there was a scraping sound behind her. Wheeling around Demi was astonished to see Ellie's mother moving towards her out of the shadows. The woman was holding a big piece of wood in her hand and swinging it towards Demi's head. Before Demi could raise her hands to protect herself, Kathleen struck. The blow was hard. Demi staggered backwards and dropped to the floor, the room turning black beneath her eyes.

When she came to, she was no longer in her house. Instead, she was in a large square-shaped room with a pull-up corrugated door. A big antique mirror hung from one of the concrete walls a few feet away. Below the mirror were a couple of work units with one or two rusty tools laying on top of the surfaces. Judging by the general size and shape of the building, Demi decided that she was probably in a storage lock-up or somebody's garage.

As she lifted her injured head to study the room in more detail, Demi realised that she'd been tied down. Her wrists and ankles had been secured onto a thick wooden bench by home-made metal clasps. Craning her ears and fighting against the grogginess that hung like a cloud beneath her eyes, she listened for outside sounds, trying to gauge her surroundings by the general noise. Outside the world was completely quiet. Nothing sounded in her ears to give her location away.

Twisting her neck sideways she thought she

saw a black shadow move inside the mirror. She stared intently at the glass but whatever had been there was gone. Maybe she was going crazy? She didn't think so. She'd seen something, she was sure of it. Goosebumps rose on her skin. The room had suddenly turned cold. Breath rose into the air from her mouth as the room cooled further.

The shadow was there again. This time she could see it clearly. She stared at the glass, watching as the black mass slowly began to take shape. The blurred figure could have belonged to a woman, but Demi couldn't be sure. The image had no face, just the contours of a rapidly changing outline. Demi glared at it unable to look away. Whatever the thing was, Demi sensed that it was evil, that it meant her harm. She could feel its malevolence as it hovered inside its glass cage, watching her, hungering.

Just as suddenly as it had started the cold snap was gone. As it lifted, the image inside the mirror melted away leaving Demi alone wondering what the hell she's just seen.

Outside the lockup, Demi could hear rapidly approaching footsteps. Whoever was coming had disturbed the thing that lay inside the mirror. The footsteps grew louder. They stopped just outside the door. Demi watched as the roller moved and the door began to slide upwards. Two figures appeared in the opening. As the two women made their way towards her bench, Demi stared in shock. Kathleen she'd been expecting, but the woman with her she hadn't. "Stohl?" she gasped letting the name escape from her lips. "You had a hand in all this?"

"Yes," Stohl said stopping beside the bench. "It's unfortunate but these things happen. Everything has gotten out of hand. You weren't supposed to be taken yet. Sadly, things have escalated beyond our control. We have had to bring everything forward."

"What the hell is this all about? What have you done with my husband?"

"Your husband is safe for now," Stohl responded. "We won't kill him as long as you do what we ask."

"Which is?"

"Come with us. Everything will be revealed."

"And if I do what you ask, you'll let Eugene go?"

Stohl had an evil glint in her eye. "Yes, we'll let him go," she laughed.

Kathleen stepped closer to the bench. One by one she unlocked the clasps on Demi's hands and feet. "Ok missy," she said helping Demi off of the wood once all four ties had been removed, "There is a car outside, get in it."

"No funny business ok! Stohl said pointing a gun. "People know we are collecting you now. If we don't arrive at our destination, Eugene will die."

"Where is he?"

"He's locked up but he's ok. That's all you need to know."

Demi stumbled out of the lock-up with Kathleen holding her tightly by the shoulders and Stohl walking on the other side of her pushing a gun into her ribs. After a short trip through a gloomy storage area, she was led over to a black Sedan parked on the kerb by the roadside. Climbing into the back seat, she waited in silence as Kathleen jumped in behind the wheel and Stohl slipped in beside her.

"It all makes sense now," she muttered as the car took off through a series of streets. "You're sending me home earlier, it was planned, wasn't it? You knew Caney would be waiting for me all along. How long have I been out anyway?"

"You've been locked up for a while," Stohl replied. "You did begin to stir around twelve this afternoon. We drugged you to keep you under. We didn't want to risk you making too much noise. As for my part in Caney threatening you, I'm afraid you couldn't be more wrong," she said shaking her head. "Ellie did that. She's been a bad little girl. It appears you have a friend. She's been trying to help you this whole time."

"So, the car being trashed, the man in my house... that was all her?" Demi said, trying to work it out in her head.

"Yeah," Stohl growled. "She called her boy-friend when she realised you were going home. She figured that if he scared you enough that you'd leave town. I don't know what the hell has gotten into her. She was primed. She was ready for the awakening. We'd picked her from all the other students because of her vulnerability. Milandra wanted her and she accepted. Since you arrived here though, it seems she has had a change of heart. The foolish girl has taken it upon herself to save you. Well, it's too late now. The moment has come. There's no escape for either of you."

Demi thought back to the moment when

she'd had the brief connection with Ellie. She'd been convinced that the girl was trying to convey a message with her eyes. The link had been severed almost as quickly as it had begun leaving Demi confused and wondering if she was losing her grip. But she'd been right after all. It seemed that Ellie had been on her side all along.

"So, what about Caney?" she asked thinking aloud. "If Ellie was trying to help me, he's not going to be so happy that you are holding me prisoner, is he?"

"Oh, I wouldn't worry about him. He's already been taken care of," Kathleen said looking at Demi through her rear-view mirror.

"He's dead, isn't he?"

Kathleen nodded.

"And Ellie?"

"She's ok. She's waiting with the others. She'll play her part in what is to come as will your husband."

"Let him go," Demi spat.

"We will, but his life won't be the same after tonight. He'll wish that we had killed him," Kathleen laughed.

"I don't understand."

"Someone killed Dean Caney," Stohl interjected, "That someone has to pay."

"You're setting him up," Demi said shaking her head in disbelief. "You're framing him for your murder. Please, you can't, he'll never survive."

"That's not my problem," Stohl said pushing the gun deeper into Demi's ribs in case she suddenly thought about doing something heroic.

After a few more winding turns, Demi realised where the car was headed. A few minutes later she was proven right. Ahead were the school gates. Heading up the short incline, the vehicle made its way over to the car park. Pulling into a vacant slot, Kathleen turned off the engine and killed the lights. Demi looked through her window. The car park was full. Cars of all shapes and sizes filled every available space.

"Get out," Stohl ordered.

Demi did as she was told. She climbed out of the car with Stohl squeezing out behind her keeping the gun trained at her body the whole time. Once Kathleen had left her seat, the two women led Demi up to reception and through the main front doors. In silence the group made their way down through the corridors, their feet echoing in the darkness. In front of the gym doors, they stopped. Kathleen indicated for Demi to move forward on her own. As she pushed the doors open, the two women fell back allowing her to lead.

The gym was packed with men and women. Demi guessed that there must be at least two hundred people gathered in the room. Some she recognised, a few teachers, the police officer that had taken her statement the day before, and some of her older pupils. Most however were strangers. All were dressed in purple robes, and each had a candle in their hand. Many were seated watching her intently as she made her way across the floor, but one or two were standing in the centre waiting for her.

In the middle of the gym where the small group was assembled, two vertical wooden beams had been erected. The beams were only a foot apart. Around the beams, a pentagram had been marked onto the floor in red chalk. Just inside the circle inches from the line, nine mirrors had been set up.

Demi stared at the nearest of the two beams. Ellie was tied to it. She was dressed in the same purple robes as the men and women around her with thick rope holding her tightly to the post.

Her face looked even paler than usual. Her eyes were dark and puffy. She looked like she'd been crying.

"I'm so sorry," Demi whispered as she was forced into a robe then bundled towards the other beam. "You tried to warn me. I understand that now."

Some of the older men in the circle held her against the wood whilst others fastened her with a tight binding. Once she was secure the men backed away.

Ellie turned her head and stared at the teacher. "Don't be afraid," she whispered. "They won't win. When this is over, you'll understand."

Demi admired the girl's courage, but the battle was already lost. They were going to die and neither one of them could do anything to save themselves.

Ellie leaned her head closer. Lowering her voice even further, she whispered something only Demi could hear. Once she'd said what she'd wanted to say, she smiled and looked away. The words were as powerful as they were shocking. Demi felt a deep surge of grief. She fought back the tears that threatened to consume her eyes. She finally understood why Ellie had looked the way she had. The makeup, the clothes, they were all camouflage to hide a secret that the girl didn't want the world to see. Hanging her head in shame, Demi waited for what was about to come.

"Men and women of the purple enclave, we stand here gathered tonight to witness the rebirth of our dark Goddess, Milandra queen of mirrors," the head of the order begun. "Tonight, her cage will be no more She will walk again amongst us, and we the anointed will know her love."

"Milandra, Milandra," the room chanted.

"Milandra, dark Goddess, queen of mirrors, come to us, accept our sacrifice and take the body we have prepared for you in this glorious realm," the man continued.

Taking a goat from a cage bought into the circle by one of his followers he slit its throat then began moving around the circle painting an upside-down cross on each of his disciples' foreheads. When all the foreheads were done, he and a helper dragged the closet mirror in front of Ellie. The mirror was heavy, but with some effort, they managed to position it in place.

"Milandra, we beseech you, come out of the prison to which you were exiled and take your throne which is rightfully yours. Accept Ellie the last of the nine. Come out of the darkness and take her body that you might live."

Picking up a big heavy black book, he began to quote a passage in Latin. As he read, the shadow that Demi had seen in the lock-up started to fill the mirror. The temperature in the gym began to plummet. Demi could feel the goosebumps rising on her skin again.

"Milandra, Milandra, Milandra," the room chanted.

As everyone watched on, a black mist began to sweep out from the glass. The mist swirled and ebbed then shot forward into Ellie's open screaming mouth. Ellie's eyes widened then turned black as all nine mirrors burst, their glass shattering into a million pieces.

"Release me," Milandra ordered the head of the order. "Unbind me from these ropes. Do it now," she snarled. The that came out of her mouth no longer belonged to Ellie. It was deeper, almost demonic.

Two of the order rushed forward and untied her. As she stepped away from the beam they dropped to their knees and bowed their heads.

"Is this my sacrifice?" Milandra said turning to look at Demi. "Yes, I have seen her. I will take her eyes," she purred. "They have looked upon me; they have seen me as I was. They must be devoured. I will take her sight as I will take the sight of all who do not adore me," she muttered.

Lunging forward she dug her nails into Demi's eye sockets and ripped out her eyeballs. As Demi screamed in agony, Milandra dropped the eyes into her mouth and began to chew. Spitting the half-eaten eyes onto the floor she suddenly staggered backwards.

"What have you done to me?" she roared. Teetering off balance she clawed at her skin as if it were on fire. "You tricked me," she screamed. "This vessel is spoilt. A disease lives within her."

"No, no that's not true," the head of the order cried out in fear. "It cannot be. We'd have known."

"Liar!" Milandra yelled out in a fit of rage. "This body is decay. You knew it but you allowed me to take it anyway. Is this your offering to me? Is this your devotion? I will destroy you all for this."

"No, you have to believe us. She tricked us all. Please, we didn't know. We only wish to love you."

"Then find me a mirror, do it now or I will

die, and you will all go to hell with me."

The room was suddenly a mass of moving bodies, everyone scrambling to find a mirror to save their God. Their efforts were in vain. It was already too late. The cancer was too deep. It had taken every part of Ellie's frail body. The girl had known it all along. The doctors had given her just days to live. Her time had finally run out.

As Milandra collapsed to the floor trapped inside the vessel that held her in its deadly embrace, she waved her arm in one last act of fury. Everyone in the room dropped down to the floor gasping for breath. Holding their throats, they jerked and spasmed as their lungs collapsed inside their chests. As Milandra took her last breath, so too did her disciples.

When the room was quiet once more and the dead lay cold upon the floor, Demi whispered a quiet thank you to Ellie.

"I've lost my eyes, but I see now," she mouthed. "I will never forget you, Ellie Krasz. I will make sure that everyone remembers you and I will honour you until my dying day..."

CYE THOMAS

COMING SOON

THE GOD BUBBLE

Prologue

In my dream, I am floating high above the world. I can feel my body, but I cannot see it. Around me billions of stars twinkle like jewels, stretching out into the vast chasm of space. I am not alone. Something is with me. It lies trapped within a small bubble that glistens like a dewdrop in the black velvet darkness. I try to look inside but every time I get near it moves away. It is toying with me playfully staying beyond my reach.

I try to follow, holding my breath as I move quietly closer, stealth my friend aiding me in my quest. Soon I am close enough to touch. I reach out but the bubble is gone denying me a glimpse of my elusive prize. I wake frustrated.

For nearly three weeks now the dream has been the same. It haunts my sleeping hours, pushing me to the farthest depths of my psyche. The dream is telling me something, talking to me like an old friend, inviting me to see, but always the answer eludes me. Again and again, I stumble like a blind man unable to understand.

Tonight, as my mind begins to drift, I realise that something has changed. I sense that my journey is almost at an end. Excitement washes over me like a gentle stream. It builds within my mind turning my sleeping thoughts into a raging river. As I have done so many times before I stretch out my hand. Electricity surges through my body. My heart thumps in my chest, but still, the bubble floats beyond my reach. For a moment I am confused. Frustration creeps into my head, but then it drops. It hurtles toward the earth below like a stone, fire engulfing its rim.

I watch as the bubble plunges through the darkness and into the atmosphere speeding through the clouds like a missile, homing in on some unknown target far below. Beneath the fire the teardrop glistens, I see it even through the flames that burn like a furnace around it. I instinctively know where it is headed and follow it down.

It is not long before I see the roof of my house. I smile as I watch the elusive membrane crash through the flimsy tiles. It lands softly on my bed. Instinctively I know what lies inside, even though it has not yet been made visible to me.

The sleeping me thrashes beneath the sheets as my waking mind peers inside, allowing me my first glimpse of the gold cage within. Staring at the brain I finally understand. I smile and open my eyes.

MORE FROM
BREAKING RULES EUROPE

Face of Fear by C. Marry Hultman
e-book:books2read.com/u/49lVg0
Paperback: mybook.to/Face-of-Fear

Dawson Junior G3 by Brian Wagstaff
e-book:books2read.com/u/4EP99E
Paperback: mybook.to/Dawson

Boy in the Wardrobe by Esther Jacoby
e-book: mybook.to/Boy-Wardrobe

New Life Cottage by Esther Jacoby
e-book:books2read.com/u/m0wAzW
Paperback: mybook.to/New-Life-Cottage

The Wait by Esther Jacoby
e-book: https://books2read.com/u/4Dgz8Q

Liebe ist Warten by Esther Jacoby
e-book:https://books2read.com/u/mZaVD2
Paperback: mybook.to/Liebe

Musing on Death & Dying by Esther Jacoby
e-book:books2read.com/u/49lVg0
Paperback: mybook.to/Musings

Earth Door by Cye Thomas
e-book:books2read.com/u/mKyXKv
Paperback: mybook.to/Earth-Door

Graffiti Stories by Nick Gerrard
e-book:books2read.com/u/m2MQOR
Paperback: mybook.to/Grafitti-Stories

Punk Novelette by Nick Gerrard
e-book:books2read.com/u/4jLpqv
Paperback: mybook.to/Punk-Novelette

Struggle and Strife by Nick Gerrard
e-book:books2read.com/u/4DRyqr
Paperback: mybook.to/struggle-strife

Fake Escape by Natalie Hughes
e-book:https://books2read.com/u/bMXL5X

Murder Planet by Adam Carpenter
e-book:books2read.com/u/bMXllV
Paperback: mybook.to/Murder-Planet

Generation Ship by Adam Carpenter
e-book:books2read.com/u/49Nk8M
Paperback: mybook.to/generation

Cold as Hell by Neen Cohen
e-book:https://books2read.com/u/bxennv
Paperback: mybook.to/Grafitti-Stories

Six Days to Hell by E.L. Giles
e-book:https://books2read.com/u/bWrLyq
Paperback: mybook.to/SixDaystoHell

Just 13 anthology
e-book: https://books2read.com/u/mKy1B9

Lost Lore & Legends Anthology
e-book:books2read.com/u/m2RrwG
Paperback: mybook.to/Lost-Lore-Legends-pbk

Find us at:
www.breakingrulespublishingeuro.com

ABOUT THE AUTHOR

Cye Thomas was born in Kent, the garden of England. He is a lyricist and has been in several bands since his early teens all of which produced their own material. In his early twenties, Cye joined the Royal Air Force and it is whilst stationed at Odiham in Hampshire that he discovered the beauty of the surrounding West country. On completion of service, he returned to his hometown where he still resides with long-term partner Helen. Cye has also written a few poems which were published back in the 1990s.

After writing his first novel he decided to write a few short stories which he admitted was in fact harder to do.

When not writing, Cye's other hobbies include martial arts and listening to all genres of music.